THE PENGUIN CLASSICS

FOUNDER EDITOR (1944–64): E. V. RIEU

IVAN SERGEYEVICH TURGENEV was born in 1818 in the Province of Orel, and suffered during his childhood from a tyrannical mother. After the family had moved to Moscow in 1827 he entered Petersburg University where he studied philosophy. When he was nineteen he published his first poems and, convinced that Europe contained the source of real knowledge, went to the University of Berlin. After two years he returned to Russia and took his degree at the University of Moscow. In 1843 he fell in love with Pauline Garcia-Viardot, a young Spanish singer, who influenced the rest of his life: he followed her on her singing tours in Europe and spent long periods in the French house of herself and her husband, both of whom accepted him as a family friend. He sent his daughter by a sempstress to be brought up among the Viardot children. After 1856 he lived mostly abroad, and he became the first Russian writer to gain a wide reputation in Europe; he was a well-known figure in Parisian literary circles, where his friends included Flaubert and the Goncourt brothers, and an honorary degree was conferred on him at Oxford. His series of six novels reflect a period of Russian life from the 1830s to the 1870s: they are *Rudin* (1855), *Home of the Gentry* (1858), *On the Eve* (1859), *Fathers and Sons* (1861), *Smoke* (1867) and *Virgin Soil* (1876). He also wrote plays, which include the comedy, *A Month in the Country*; short stories and *Sketches from a Hunter's Album* (a Penguin Classic); and literary essays and memories. He died in Paris in 1883 after being ill for a year, and was buried in Russia.

ON THE EVE

A NOVEL BY I. S. TURGENEV

Translated by Gilbert Gardiner

PENGUIN BOOKS

Penguin Books Ltd, Harmondsworth, Middlesex, England
Penguin Books, 625 Madison Avenue, New York, New York 10022, U.S.A.
Penguin Books Australia Ltd, Ringwood, Victoria, Australia
Penguin Books Canada Ltd, 2801 John Street, Markham, Ontario, Canada L3R 1B4
Penguin Books (N.Z.) Ltd, 182–190 Wairau Road, Auckland 10, New Zealand

—

First published 1950
Reprinted 1967, 1972, 1973, 1976, 1977, 1979, 1981

—

Copyright 1950 by Gilbert Gardiner
All rights reserved

—

Set, printed and bound in Great Britain by
Cox & Wyman Ltd, Reading
Set in Monotype Bembo

CONTENTS

IVAN SERGEYEVICH
TURGENEV

*

Born 1818, in Oryol, Central Russia
Died 1883, in Paris

INTRODUCTION

WHEN Turgenev was a child he lived with his mother and father and elder brother in the manor-house at Spasskoye, in the province of Oryol, south-west of Moscow. It was an immense house of forty rooms, with endless corridors, secret staircases and dark corners, and it was surrounded by a great garden. One night, when he was still quite small, Turgenev determined to run away.

'I got up and dressed quietly,' he tells us, 'and crept down the corridor in the darkness to the hall. I did not even know where I wanted to go; I only felt that I must run away so that no one would find me, and that this was my only hope of salvation ... Suddenly a lighted candle appeared in the corridor, and I saw to my horror someone approaching me – it was my German tutor. He seized me by the arm in great astonishment, and began to question me.

'"I want to run away," I told him, breaking into tears.

'"What, where to?"

'"Wherever I can."

'"What for?"

'"Because they keep thrashing me, and I don't know why."

'"You don't know why?"

'"I swear to God I don't know."

'At this the good-natured old gentleman began to caress me and embrace me, and he promised me they would not punish me any more.'

If we look to Turgenev's childhood for a clue to his later

7

development, we may find enlightenment in the harsh treatment he received in his early years. His mother ruled her children, as she ruled her serfs, with tyrannical severity. It is said that the children were thrashed for some trifle almost every day.

During this early period his only happiness was in the grounds and countryside surrounding Spasskoye. He knew every corner of the immense garden: the tree beneath which he had found the giant mushroom, the scene of the battle between the slow-worm and the frog, the two handsome pine trees growing side by side on the lawn, the lake, the orchard – everything was dear to him here. In later life he never lost his love of nature, and his novels are famous for their charming descriptions of the countryside.

When he was nine years old he was sent to a boarding-school in Moscow, and six years later he entered Moscow University, the institution of which Bersyenev, in *On the Eve*, remarked: 'It is a school, not a university.' Possibly this was also Turgenev's view; at any rate, after a year he moved on to St Petersburg University and entered the 'historico-philological' faculty there. The teaching was no better than at Moscow, but he read voraciously and began to write verses.

This was the time of Pushkin, and the great age of Russian literature was beginning. Russian literature of the nineteenth century was comparable in the suddenness of its emergence with the English literature of the Elizabethans. Before Pushkin (1799–1837) there had hardly been a Russian literature; now, in the early thirties, Gogol and Lermontov were already writing, Turgenev was growing up, Tolstoy and Dostoyevsky were children. For Turgenev at this time Pushkin was a demigod and his admiration for the poet lasted till the end of his life.

A year after taking his degree at St Petersburg he went abroad, and spent the next few years travelling in Europe and studying in Berlin. He led the carefree existence of the well-to-do student of those days: a life of endless conversations and ardent friendships, of music and art, of love-making and sightseeing. Berlin University was then the centre of Hegelian teaching, and Turgenev's principal interest was philosophy; but politics occupied him too, and his liberal ideas gathered strength in the society of the intellectuals among whom he moved. He became acquainted with Michael Bakunin, and a warm friendship sprang up between the future novelist and the future anarchist.

Like Bersyenev in the novel, Turgenev had dreams of becoming a professor of philosophy, and when he returned to Russia he began to study with this object in view. However, the plan came to nothing, and he took, instead, a position in the Ministry of the Interior. The life of a civil servant did not prove much to his liking, and he gave it up after two years; but in the meantime he was writing, and in 1843 he published *Parasha, a Story in Verse*. When, to his astonishment, he read an article in warm praise of the poem by the great critic Belinsky, he was – characteristically – more embarrassed than delighted. Turgenev was always curiously lacking in confidence as to the value of his own work.

Belinsky was the central figure in a group of Petersburg writers and thinkers which included Nekrassov and Dostoyevsky, Annenkov and Grigorovich, Druzhinin and Botkin, men of diverse talents, tastes and social origins who were united in their opposition to the system of serfdom and who looked to western Europe for a pattern for the future development of Russia. In this circle Turgenev quickly became a general favourite. 'This is an unusually intelligent man, and in general a good man too,' Belinsky wrote of him. 'Conversation and disputation with him bring me consolation . . . There's anger and spite and bitterness in him . . .' And Dostoyevsky wrote of him at that time: 'A poet, a man of talent, an aristocrat, handsome, rich, clever, cultured – I don't know what nature has denied him.'

In 1847 Turgenev scored his first big literary success. Panayev, editor of the magazine *Contemporary*, was looking for something to fill up his 'miscellany'; Turgenev, who had just decided to abandon literature – a decision he made many times in the course of his life – gave Panayev a prose sketch to help him out. Its publication at once brought Turgenev fame and acclamation. *Khor and Kalinich*, as it was called, was destined to be the first of a considerable series of descriptive pieces which were known collectively as the *Sportsman's Sketches* and which took as their theme the life of the peasantry and country gentry. The next pieces in the series, however, were written abroad, as Turgenev left Russia for Berlin early in 1847.

While the publication of *Khor and Kalinich* was a turning point in Turgenev's literary career, the event which most profoundly influenced his personal life had occurred some years earlier: this was when he met Pauline Viardot, a celebrated opera singer of Spanish descent who was performing in St Petersburg at the time. From then onwards Turgenev's passion for the singer seems to have dominated his life. The relationship was apparently platonic, and in return for his love she gave him only her friendship and regard; but in later life he settled down with her and became accepted by her husband and children almost as one of the family; he moved his abode when she moved hers, he even arranged for her to adopt and educate the illegitimate daughter he had had by a Russian sewing-woman. When he died it was as an old bachelor in her care.

It was in furtherance of this extraordinary liaison that he went abroad in 1847, at the age of twenty-nine, and for the next three years he was mainly in Paris, where the Viardots were living. For Turgenev this was a period of great literary activity, the most productive period of his life. 'Not a week passes,' he wrote at one point, 'that I don't send off a large packet to Russia.' He wrote most of the *Sportsman's Sketches* and several plays, including the well-known comedy *A Month in the Country*. His dramatic work did much to revive the contemporary Russian theatre, though all his life Turgenev was persuaded that his plays were not 'scenic', and could only 'offer a certain interest' when read.

He returned to Russia in 1850, and in the same year his gifted, sadistic, eccentric mother died. He had quarrelled with her, and was not present at her death. Later he found her diary, and, having read it through, wrote to Madame Viardot: 'What a woman, my friend, what a woman! I couldn't close my eyes all night. May God pardon her for everything! . . . Really, I feel quite shaken.' The death of his mother left Turgenev a wealthy man, though all his life he was to suffer from financial embarrassments on account of his unbusinesslike methods and character.

Another death, that of Gogol, the novelist and playwright, affected him profoundly, and led to rather far-reaching consequences.

Towards the middle of the last century the censorship in Russia reached an unprecedented level of severity and absurdity (even musical compositions were suspect, for fear the notes might form some kind of cipher). Now it was Turgenev's turn to offend the authorities, and to suffer for his indiscretion. Under the first impact of Gogol's death in

1852, he wrote a short article for the *St Petersburg Gazette*: 'Gogol is dead! . . . What Russian heart is not shaken by those three words? . . . He is gone, that man whom we now have the right, the bitter right given to us by death, to call great.' It is said that Turgenev sobbed as he wrote those lines, but, however that may be, the St Petersburg censor would not pass the article for publication. The government, for political reasons, wanted to play down Gogol's death; the censor thought it unbecoming 'to write about his death in such a pompous manner . . . and to present his death as an irreparable loss'. At this Turgenev sent the article to Moscow, where the censor, unaware of the St Petersburg decision, permitted its publication. As a result of this, Turgenev was imprisoned in the capital for a month and then 'exiled' to his estate for nearly two years.

During his long sojourn in the country, Turgenev's thoughts turned increasingly to the composition of a full-length novel. 'I must take another road,' he wrote soon after the publication of the collected *Sportsman's Sketches*, 'I must find it and take leave of the old manner for ever. I have been trying sufficiently long to extract the concentrated essences from human character – the *triples extraits* – in order to pour them into small bottles for my esteemed readers to sniff at . . . but the question is, am I capable of anything big and calm?' His question was answered equivocally by his first novel, *Rudin* (1855), but with a resounding affirmative by his second, *A House of Gentlefolk*, which at once established him as the leading writer of the day. No other novel of his ever achieved such popularity or esteem. He was lionized on all sides; left-wing and right-wing critics approved; eminent men strove for his friendship, young writers brought him their manuscripts for judgement. Herzen, in London, described him as 'the greatest contemporary Russian artist'. Replying to this, Turgenev wrote: 'I feel ashamed, and I couldn't believe it, but I liked it.'

According to an inscription on the manuscript title-page, the plan of *A House of Gentlefolk* was conceived at the beginning of 1856, but the author 'did not set to work on it for a long time, while continually turning it over in his mind': then he started to write it in the summer of 1858 and finished it in a few months. This long gestation and short labour were often characteristic of Turgenev's creative method, and particularly so in the case of his next novel, *On the Eve*. The idea for this story came to him in 1854 or 1855, and he returned to it from time to time during the ensuing years, but the final plan was formed only in the spring of 1859; then the actual writing of the story took only about six months.

On the Eve aroused intense interest when it appeared in *The Russian Herald*, but it did not win the universal applause which had been accorded to its predecessor. It is essentially a love story with a historical background, told with consummate skill, moving inevitably to its tragic conclusion and rich in brilliant characterizations. To the Russians, however, the social and political implications of the novel were deeply significant; and, indeed, the very title of the book has a political flavour, being short for 'On the Eve of Reform'. People argued about the heroes of the story as they might have done about real people – about their characters, their conduct and their importance to Russia. Even quite recently, during the war years, a Russian critic wrote: 'To the reader of our days the thoughts of the author and the images of his characters are no less near or dear than they were to Turgenev's contemporaries. To us the noble aspirations and the experiences of Insarov, fired as he was with deep love of his mother-country, are near and intelligible . . .' Perhaps the book has something to teach us also about Russian aspirations and attitudes.

On the Eve was the first important work by Turgenev which did not appear in the *Contemporary*. In the early days of his association with this magazine he had been an influential figure in its editorial policy, which reflected the views of the liberal gentry; in the middle 'fifties, however, the editorial circle was joined by two young critics, Chernishevski and Dobrolyubov, who held strongly radical opinions, and who gradually came to dominate its pages. To Turgenev their politics were too revolutionary, for he was a believer in gradual reform; and their views on art were shocking, for they saw in it only a means to an end, while he believed passionately that art was an ultimate value. The breach widened, and in 1860 he finally dissociated himself from the magazine.

It is significant of Turgenev's divided attitude of mind that he should have utilized his knowledge of Dobrolyubov and Chernishevski, with whom he had quarrelled on matters of principle, in creating the character of Bazarov, the hero of his next book – a character he seems to have admired. Turgenev created Bazarov not, like so many of his characters, in his own image, but in defiance of it. This was the most powerful of Turgenev's full-length figures, the strong-willed 'man of action', whom he had sought to depict in *On the Eve* with only partial success; and *Fathers and Children*, the novel in which he appears, is widely regarded as Turgenev's finest work. Yet, in spite of the sensation which its publication in 1861 caused, it was not warmly received and his reputation suffered, particularly with the younger radicals. He himself, always highly sensitive to the opinions of his friends, even contemplated burning the manuscript before it was printed. He was deeply disappointed with its reception, and wrote very little in the years which immediately followed its publication.

For many years Turgenev had made regular journeys abroad, and in 1862 he left Russia for good, returning to his native land only for short visits. Henceforth his life was outwardly uneventful, the life of an established literary man whose most important work was already accomplished. Readers of *On the Eve* may be surprised, and possibly affronted, to find one of the characters described as an 'old man' of 'nearly fifty'; but this was very much Turgenev's attitude towards himself. He was only forty-three when he settled abroad, but already he felt that his years of achievement were passed; and although he was still to write a great deal, and much that was of value, it is true that none of his subsequent novels achieved the stature of the work he had done before he left Russia.

'If the Viardot family moved to Australia,' Turgenev used to say, 'I would go after them.' In fact they moved to Baden-Baden, and the small Black Forest town became his home also. These were placid years. He found happiness in the society of Madame Viardot and her family, in music and amateur operatics, in hunting with Monsieur Viardot and with his faithful dog Pegasus. Yet his underlying state of mind was melancholy. He sensed the approach of old age; he felt that he was cut off from Russia and that this must harm his effectiveness as a writer; he suffered from hypochondria. His most important production during the Baden period was the novel *Smoke*, in which he satirized both the reactionary aristocrats and the radicals. Of the reception of this novel he said that everyone abused him, 'the reds and the whites, from above and below and the side'; . . . 'no one had ever been abused with such unanimity' as he was for *Smoke*.

After the Franco-Prussian war the Viardot family settled in Paris, and Turgenev went to live with them in their house in the rue de Douai. His life, continuing placidly as before, was enriched by his friendships with many of the leading French writers – particularly Flaubert, E. Goncourt, Daudet and Zola. The five arranged regular dinners together – 'the dinners of the authors who have been hissed' as they were called. With his great Russian contemporaries, Dostoyevsky and Tolstoy, he had quarrelled, though there was a reconciliation with Tolstoy at the end.

In spite of his frequent decisions to give up literature, Turgenev continued to write until the end of his life. *Virgin Soil*, a novel dealing with a revolutionary movement of the time, was completed when he was fifty-eight; in his last years he wrote the *Poems in Prose*, he continued to produce sketches and articles, he added to the large collection of short stories which already stood to his name. Shortly before his death, when he was too ill to hold a pen, he dictated a story to Madame Viardot. He died in August, 1883, at the age of sixty-four, in Bougival, a suburb of Paris.

Towards the end of his life Turgenev's reputation in Russia had been reviving, and when he returned to Moscow and St Petersburg in 1879, his visit was the occasion for celebrations and demonstrations in his honour. Although his personal achievement as a writer and artist was recognized in the triumph which he enjoyed, there is no doubt that the demonstrations also had a political background. 'I realize that they are not honouring me,' he said, 'but that they're using me as a stick with which to beat the government.' Yet, however important the political and sociological aspect of Turgenev's work may have been to his contemporaries and to himself, to us it is only of minor significance. To us it is Turgenev the artist who is important, the Turgenev with the masterly narrative power, with the exquisite sense of style and the sure sense of character – the Turgenev of whom it has been written:

'Any one who goes back to his books after a time, and after a course of more modern and rougher, stormier literature will, I think, be surprised at its excellence and perhaps be inclined to heave a deep sigh of relief. Some of it will appear conventional; he will notice a faint atmosphere of rose-water; he will feel, if he has been reading the moderns, as a traveller feels who, after an exciting but painful journey, through dangerous ways and unpleasant surroundings, suddenly enters a cool garden, where fountains sob between dark cypresses, and swans float majestically on artificial lakes. There is an aroma of syringa in the air; the pleasaunce is artistically laid out, and full of fragrant flowers. But he will not despise that garden for its elegance and its tranquil seclusion, for its trees cast large shadows, the nightingale sings in its thickets, the moon silvers the calm statues, and the sound of music on the waters goes to the heart. Turgenev reminds one of a certain kind of music, beautiful in form, not too passionate and yet full of emotion, Schumann's music, for instance; if Pushkin is the Mozart of Russian literature, Turgenev is the Schumann; not amongst the very greatest, but still a poet, full of inspired lyrical feeling; and a great, a classic artist, the prose Virgil of Russian literature.'*   G. G.

* Quoted from *Russian Literature*, by Maurice Baring (Home University Library). See *Turgenev*, by A. Yarmolinsky (London, Hodder & Stoughton, 1926); *The Life of Turgenev*, by L. S. Utyevski (included in *Turgenev's Selected Works*, Moscow, 1941); 'Introduction', by N. Kalitin, to an edition of *On the Eve* (Moscow, 1944).

THE PRINCIPAL CHARACTERS

NIKOLAI ARTYOMEVICH STAHOV: a retired lieutenant of the guards.

ANNA VASSILYEVNA: his wife.

ELENA NIKOLAYEVNA: their daughter. (Familiar name: Lenochka.)

UVAR IVANOVICH STAHOV: a distant uncle of Nikolai Artyomevich.

PAVEL YAKOVLEVICH SHUBIN: a young sculptor, related to Anna Vassilyevna. (In French: 'Paul'.)

ANDREI PETROVICH BERSYENEV: a student of philosophy, graduate of Moscow University.

DMITRI NIKANOROVICH INSAROV: a Bulgarian student.

ZOYA NIKITISHNA MUELLER: companion to Elena Nikolayevna.

AVGUSTINA CHRISTIANOVNA: a widow, mistress of Nikolai Artyomevich.

YEGOR ANDREYEVICH KURNATOVSKI: a chief secretary at the Senate.

THE HISTORICAL BACKGROUND

The main action of the story takes place between the summer of 1853 and the spring of 1854. The Crimean War broke out early in 1854, but tension between Russia on the one hand and Turkey, Great Britain and France, on the other, had been growing during the preceding year, Russian troops had occupied the Principalities of Moldavia and Wallachia, which formed roughly what we know as Rumania today, and Turkey, at the beginning of October, 1853, demanded that Russia should withdraw her troops within fifteen days (page 190). Soon afterwards, Turkish troops crossed the Danube into Wallachia, and hostilities broke out between Turkey and Russia. Efforts at mediation were still being made when, on November 30th, the Russian fleet attacked and destroyed a Turkish squadron in the Black Sea; this event, known as the 'Massacre of Sinope', led to the entry of the British and French fleets into the Black Sea. Negotiations broke down in February, 1854, and war between Russia and the Western powers became unavoidable.

I

It was one of the hottest days of the summer of 1853. By the side of the Moscow River, not far from Kuntsovo, two young men were lying on the grass in the shade of a tall lime tree.

One of them looked about twenty-three years of age; he was tall and dark-complexioned and had a rather crooked, pointed nose and a high forehead. There was a restrained smile on his full lips, and he was screwing up his small grey eyes a trifle as he gazed meditatively into the distance.

The other was lying on his chest, propping up his fair curly head with both hands and gazing likewise into the distance. He was three years older than his companion, but he seemed much younger; his moustache hardly showed and there was a light curly down on his chin. In the small features of his fresh, round face, in his soft brown eyes and prominent, well-shaped lips, in his small white hands, there was an engaging elegance and something of the prettiness of a child. Everything about him seemed to breathe the joy, the gaiety of health, everything breathed youth – carefree, self-confident, charming, pampered youth. He rolled his eyes and he smiled and he propped up his head in the manner of a boy who knows that people take pleasure in looking at him. He was wearing a loose white coat like a blouse, and a light blue scarf was wrapped round his slender neck. A crumpled straw hat was lying in the grass beside him.

Compared with him his companion seemed an old man, and no one looking at his angular figure would have thought that he too was enjoying himself and at his ease. He lay in an awkward attitude; his big head, broad at the top and narrowing at the base, sat awkwardly on his long neck. Clumsiness was expressed in the very posture of his arms, of his long legs, with their knees raised like the hind legs of a dragon-fly, of his body in its short, tightly-fitting black jacket. Yet, in spite of all that, one could not but recognize in him a cultured person; his whole awkward being bore the imprint of 'respectability', and his face, plain and even rather laughable though it was, expressed a habitual thoughtfulness and kindliness. Andrei Petrovich Bersyenev was his name; that of his companion, the fair-haired young man, Pavel Yakovlevich Shubin.

'Why don't you lie on your front, as I do?' Shubin began. 'It's much better like that. Especially when you lift up your legs and knock your heels together – like that. You've got the grass under your nose; if you get tired of staring at the landscape, you can look at some pot-bellied beetle crawling along a blade of grass, or an ant bustling about. It really is better. But you've taken up a sort of pseudo-classical pose, just like a ballet dancer resting her elbows on a cardboard rock. You should remember that you are now perfectly entitled to relax. It's no joke, coming out third in the finals! Rest, sir; take it easy, stretch your limbs!'

Shubin said all this through his nose half-indolently, half in fun – as spoilt children speak to friends of the family who bring them sweets. Then without waiting for an answer he continued:

'What strikes me most about ants and beetles and other gentlemen of the insect world is their astonishing seriousness: they run backwards and forwards with such important expressions on their faces, just as if their life really meant something. Just think: Man, Lord of Creation, most exalted of beings, is looking at them – but they've no time for him; what's more, a gnat will sit on the nose of the Lord of the Creation and use him for food. It's insulting. Yet, looked at in another way, how is our life any better than theirs? And why shouldn't they give themselves airs, if we are permitted to do so? Now then, my philosopher, solve that problem for me. Why don't you answer? Eh?'

'What?' said Bersyenev, with a start.

'What!' repeated Shubin. 'Your friend expounds his profound ideas to you and you don't listen.'

'I was admiring the view. Look at the hot glow of those fields in the sun' (Bersyenev spoke with a slight lisp).

'Yes, there's been a lot of magnificent colour splashed about,' Shubin said. 'That's nature for you!'

Bersyenev shook his head.

'You ought to be even more enraptured by all this sort of thing than I am. This is in your line: you're an artist.'

'No, sir, this is not in my line,' Shubin retorted, putting his hat on the back of his head. 'I am a butcher, sir. My business is flesh, to model flesh – shoulders, arms, legs. Here there is no form, no completeness; everything sprawls all over the place – you just try to get hold of it!'

'Still, there's beauty here too, you know,' Bersyenev said. 'By the way, did you finish your *bas-relief*?'

'Which?'

'The child and goat.'

'To Hell with that, to Hell with that,' Shubin chanted. 'I looked at the real thing, at the old masters, at the classics – and I smashed up my own rubbish. You show me nature and you say "There's beauty here, too". Yes, of course, there's beauty in everything, there's even beauty in your nose, but you can't try to capture every kind of beauty. The old masters – they didn't run after beauty; it just came into their work, God knows where from – from heaven, maybe. All the world belonged to them, but we can't spread ourselves like that; our reach is too short. We cast our line to a single point and watch and wait. If there's a bite, that's fine! If not . . .'

Shubin put out his tongue.

'Stop, stop,' Bersyenev interrupted. 'That's a paradox. If you don't respond to beauty, if you don't love it wherever you meet it, beauty will elude you even in your art. If a lovely view or beautiful music doesn't speak to your heart – I mean, if you don't respond to them –'

'Oh, you responder,' Shubin burst out, laughing at his new word; but Bersyenev was pensive.

'No, my friend,' Shubin continued, 'you're a clever fellow, a philosopher, third graduate at Moscow University, and it's too frightening arguing with you, especially for a half-educated student like me. But this I will tell you: apart from my art, I love beauty only in women, in young women – and that only lately.'

He turned over on his back and put his hands behind his head. For some moments neither spoke. The sultry silence of noon hung oppressively over the glowing, slumbering earth.

'Apropos of women,' Shubin began again, 'why doesn't someone take Stahov in hand? Did you see him in Moscow?'

'No.'

'The old fellow is completely out of his mind. All day long he's round at his Avgustina Christianovna's; he's bored stiff, but there he sits. They gaze at one another so stupidly – it's really nauseating to see it. Just think of it – what a family God blessed that man with! – but no, he must have Avgustina Christianovna. I've never seen anything more hideous than her duck-like face. The other day I modelled a caricature of her in the Dantan manner. It wasn't at all bad. I'll show it to you.'

'And the bust of Elena Nikolayevna,' Bersyenev asked, 'is it progressing?'

'No, my friend, it's not progressing. That face could drive you to despair. You look at it: clean lines, severe, direct – you'd think it would be easy to get the likeness. But nothing of the sort – it slips through your fingers like enchanted gold. Have you noticed how she listens to you? Not a feature moves, just the expression in her eyes keeps changing, and that changes her whole face. What do you expect a sculptor to do – and a bad one at that? She's an astonishing creature . . . a strange creature,' he added after a short silence.

'Yes, she's an astonishing girl,' Bersyenev repeated after him.

'And a daughter of Nikolai Artyomevich Stahov! Talk about blood and breeding after that! And the funny thing is that she just is his daughter, she looks like him, and like her mother, Anna Vassilyevna, too. I respect Anna Vassilyevna with all my heart, indeed she's been my benefactress – but really she's a hen. Then where does Elena get her spirit? Who kindled the fire? There's another problem for you, philosopher!'

But as before, the 'philosopher' answered nothing. Bersyenev was not usually given to garrulity, and when he spoke he expressed himself awkwardly, haltingly, with needless gestures; and now a peculiar quietness had entered his soul, a quietness akin to fatigue, to melancholy. He had recently moved out of the city after long and arduous work, which had occupied him for hours every day. Now, idleness, the softness and purity of the air, the consciousness of a purpose achieved, the whimsical, casual talk with his friend, the suddenly evoked image of a charming personality, all these various and yet somehow similar impressions fused into one general sensation which soothed and agitated and weakened . . . He was a very highly-strung young man.

Under the lime tree it was cool and peaceful; the bees and flies, when they flew into the circle of its shade, seemed to hum more softly; the clean, slender blades of grass, emerald green with no glint of the sunshine's gold, were still; tall stalks stood motionless, as if bewitched; lifeless, the small clusters of yellow flowers hung from the lower branches of the tree. With every breath a sweet scent seemed to force its way into the lungs, and the lungs drank it up. Far away, beyond the river to the horizon, everything shone and glowed. Sometimes a breeze would stir there and break and intensify the glare; the radiant haze would shimmer above the earth. There was no sound of birds; they do not sing in the heat of the day. But the crickets were chirping everywhere, and it was pleasant to sit at peace in the cool shade and hear that hot sound of life; it inclined to drowsiness and induced dreams.

'Have you noticed,' Bersyenev began suddenly, helping out his words with gestures, 'what a queer feeling Nature arouses in us? In Nature, everything is so complete, so lucid – I mean so *self-satisfying* – and we appreciate all that, and admire it; yet at the same time – at least, in me – it always awakens a certain feeling of unrest, anxiety, even of sadness. What does it all mean? Either we are more conscious of our incompleteness, our vagueness when we come face to face with Nature; or else we lack the kind of harmony which satisfies Nature – while the other kind, I mean the kind that we need, Nature hasn't got.'

'Hm,' Shubin retorted, 'I'll tell you the cause of all this, Andrei Petrovich. What you have been describing are the sensations of a lonely individual who doesn't really live, but simply looks on and is overcome by his feelings. What's the good of *looking*? Live, and be a man. No matter how often you knock at Nature's door, she won't answer in words you can understand – for Nature is dumb. She'll vibrate and moan like a violin string, but you mustn't expect a song. A living soul, *that* will respond to you – above all a woman's soul. And so, my dear sir, I recommend you to get yourself a soul-mate, then all your melancholy sensations will vanish. That is what we "need", to use your own word. You see, this restlessness, this sadness – it's really just a sort of hunger. Give your belly the right stuff to eat, and everything will straighten itself out. Take your place in space as a physical body, my friend. And this "Nature", what is it, what's it for? Listen for yourself: Love . . . what a warm strong word! Nature . . . how cold and pedantic. Therefore I say' (Shubin chanted) '"Here's to Marya Petrovna" . . . or maybe not her' – he added – 'not Marya Petrovna, it really doesn't matter! You know what I mean.'

Bersyenev sat up and leaned his chin on his folded hands.

'Why the sneer?' he said, not looking at his friend. 'Why the mocking tone? Yes, you're right. Love is a great word, a great feeling . . . but what kind of love are you talking about?'

Shubin also sat up.

'What kind of love? Whatever kind you like, so long as it's love. For my part I confess that there just aren't different sorts of love. If you fall in love . . .'

'With all your soul,' Bersyenev interrupted.

'Well, of course, that goes without saying; your soul isn't an apple, you can't divide it up. If you fall in love, then you can't go wrong. But I didn't mean to jeer. There's such a tenderness in my soul just now, I feel quite soft-hearted . . . I only wanted to explain why you think Nature affects us in that way. It's because it awakens the need for love, but is not capable of satisfying it. It drives us gently into other, living arms, but we don't realize this, and expect something from Nature herself. Oh, Andrei, Andrei, how lovely this sunshine is, and that sky too, everything, everything around us is lovely, and yet you're grieving. But if at this moment you were holding the hand of a woman you loved, if that hand and all of her were yours, if you even saw with her eyes and felt, not with your own lonely feelings, but with hers – then, Andrei, it wouldn't be grief and anxiety that Nature stirred up in you, you wouldn't stop to contemplate its beauty; no, you'd find Nature itself would exult and sing, it would echo your own rhapsodies – because you would have given to Nature, dumb Nature, a tongue.'

Shubin jumped up and paced backwards and forwards once or twice; Bersyenev lowered his head and his face coloured slightly.

'I don't altogether agree with you,' he began. 'Nature isn't always hinting at . . . love' (he paused at the word), 'It threatens us also; it reminds us of awful – yes, unfathomable mysteries. Isn't it Nature that is going to devour us – isn't she always devouring us? In Nature there is Life and Death, and Death speaks as loudly as Life.'

'In Love there is Life and Death,' Shubin put in.

'And then,' Bersyenev continued, 'for instance, when I'm in the forest in the Spring, in some dense green part,

28

and I seem to hear the romantic sound of Oberon's horn'
– Bersyenev seemed a little ashamed to say this – 'is this
also –'

'It's the thirst for love, for happiness, nothing else,'
Shubin interrupted. 'I know those sounds too, and I know
that emotion, that sense of expectation which descends on
the soul in the shadow of the trees in the heart of the forest
or in the open fields, in the evening, when the sun is going
down and the mist rises from the river beyond the brush-
wood. But I expect happiness, I demand happiness, from
the forest and the river and the earth and the sky and from
every little cloud and blade of grass: I feel it coming close
to me in everything and hear its call. "My God is a bright
and joyous God." I started a poem like that once. You
must admit it's a grand first line, but I just couldn't think
of the next one. Happiness, happiness! So long as we have
life, so long as we have power over our limbs, so long as
we're climbing the hill and not coming down it! Why,
damn it!' Shubin went on with a sudden outburst: 'We're
young, we're not monsters, not fools: we'll conquer happiness for ourselves.'

He shook his curly head and looked up self-confidently,
almost defiantly at the sky.

Bersyenev glanced up at him.

'Mightn't there be something higher than happiness?'
he said quietly.

'For example?' Shubin asked and waited.

'Well, for example, you and I, as you say, we're young
and sound, let us suppose: each wants happiness for himself . . . But this word "happiness", is it the sort of word to
unite us, to fire us, to compel us to join hands in friendship?
Isn't it a selfish word, I mean a word that keeps people
apart?'

'And do you know any words that unite?'

'Yes; and they're not rare either; you know them too.'

'Well, then? What are they?'

'Well, art, at any rate – since you're an artist – then motherland, science, freedom, justice.'

'And love?' Shubin asked.

'Love unites also – but not the love you're thirsting for now: not love the pleasure, but love the sacrifice.'

Shubin frowned.

'That's all right for the Germans: but I want love for myself: I want to be number one.'

'Number one,' Bersyenev repeated. 'Whereas I feel that one's whole destiny in life should be to make oneself number two.'

'If everyone behaved as you recommend,' Shubin said, pulling a face in protest, 'there'd be no one at all to eat the pine-apples – everyone would leave them for someone else.'

'That merely means pine-apples are not necessities; however, you needn't worry – there will always be people glad to take even the bread out of other people's mouths.'

The two friends were silent for a while.

'I met Insarov again the other day,' Bersyenev began. 'I asked him to come and see me. I'm determined he must meet you . . . and the Stahovs too.'

'Who is this Insarov? Oh yes – that Serb or Bulgarian you were telling me about? That patriot? Is it he, by any chance, who's been putting all these philosophical ideas into your head?'

'Maybe.'

'He's quite a remarkable sort of person, then?'

'Yes.'

'Intelligent? Talented?'

'Intelligent? ... Yes. Talented? I don't know, I don't think so.'

'No? Then what's remarkable about him?'

'You'll see yourself. And now I think it's time for us to go. Anna Vassilyevna is probably waiting for us. What's the time?'

'Gone two. Let's go. How sultry it is! This conversation has fired my blood. And there was a moment when you ... I'm not an artist for nothing; I notice everything. Admit it, there's a woman on your mind?'

Shubin wanted to look his friend in the face, but Bersyenev turned away and walked out from under the lime tree. Shubin followed closely after him, stepping out with an easy, graceful swagger on his small feet. Bersyenev moved clumsily, lifting his shoulders high as he walked, and stretching out his neck. Yet with all that he seemed a man of better breeding than Shubin – more of a gentleman we should say, if we had not so debased the word.

II

THE young men went down to the Moscow River and walked along the bank. A cool air was wafted from the water, and the soft lapping of the small waves sounded musically in their ears.

'I'd like to bathe,' Shubin observed, 'but I'm afraid of being late. Look at the river; she seems to be luring us in. The old Greeks would have known her for a nymph – but we're no Greeks, O nymph! We're thick-skinned Scythians.'

'We have the water-sprites,' Bersyenev observed.

'You can have your water-sprites! What use are they to me, a sculptor – those offspring of a frightened, chilled imagination, creatures born in a stuffy peasant's hut in the darkness of a winter's night? – I need light and space . . . My God, when shall I get to Italy? When . . .'

'By which you mean the Ukraine?'

'For shame on you, Andrei Petrovich, blaming me for a piece of thoughtless folly – I regret it bitterly enough without that. Oh yes, I behaved like a fool: Anna Vassilyevna, kindest of women, gives me the money for the journey to Italy, and I go off among the Ukrainians and eat their dumplings and . . .'

'Don't finish it, please,' Bersyenev interrupted.

'All the same, I maintain that that money wasn't spent for nothing. Such types I saw there, especially women . . . But, of course, I know it: outside Italy there's no salvation!'

'You'll go to Italy,' Berysenev said, without turning towards him, 'and you won't do anything. You'll flap your wings but you won't fly. Don't we know you?'

'Stavasser★ flew – and he wasn't the only one. But if I don't fly, that shows I'm a penguin and don't have any wings. I'm stifled here, I want to go to Italy,' Shubin went on. 'There's sunshine there, and beauty.'

At this point a girl wearing a broad-brimmed straw hat, with a pink sunshade over her shoulder, appeared on the path along which the two friends were walking.

'But what do I see? Beauty comes to meet us even here! A humble artist salutes the enchanting Zoya!' Shubin cried suddenly, brandishing his hat with a theatrical gesture.

The girl at whom this outburst was directed stopped and shook her finger at him threateningly – then having allowed the two friends to approach her, she said with a melodious and slightly guttural voice:

'How's this, gentlemen, aren't you coming in to dinner? The table's laid.'

'What's this I hear?' Shubin said, throwing up his arms. 'Can it be that the exquisite Zoya has decided to come and look for us in all this heat? Am I to understand your remark in that sense? Tell me, do – or no, you'd better not say it; remorse would slay me on the spot.'

'Oh, stop it, Pavel Yakovlevich,' the girl retorted, not without annoyance. 'Why don't you ever talk seriously to me? I shall get cross,' she added, pouting coquettishly.

'You won't get cross with me, Zoya Nikitishna, my ideal – you wouldn't want to cast me into the black pit of uttermost despair. But as for talking seriously, I can't, for I'm not a serious person.'

★ P. A. Stavasser, a contemporary Russian sculptor.

The girl shrugged her shoulders and turned to Bersyenev.

'He always talks like that: treats me like a child, and me eighteen years old already! I'm grown-up now.'

'Oh God!' groaned Shubin, rolling his eyes upwards, while Bersyenev smiled in silence.

The girl stamped her foot.

'Pavel Yakovlevich! I shall be cross . . . Elena was going to come too,' she went on, 'but she stayed in the garden. The heat scared her, but I'm not afraid of the heat. Come let's go.'

She set off up the path, swinging her slim body slightly with each step, and brushing long locks of soft hair from her face with her small, well-shaped, black-mittened hand.

The friends followed her, Shubin now pressing his hands silently to his heart, now raising them above his head in mock admiration; a few moments later they emerged suddenly before one of the numerous villas which lie around Kuntsovo. A small wooden house, built like a chalet and painted pink, stood in the middle of the garden and peered out with a sort of naïve air from behind the greenery of the trees. Zoya, leading the way, opened the gate and ran into the garden: 'I've brought the wanderers home,' she cried. A girl with a pale expressive countenance got up from a bench by the path; then at the doorway of the house an older woman appeared. She was wearing a mauve silk dress, and covered her head with an embroidered cambric scarf as a protection from the sun, she gave them a languid, tired smile.

III

ANNA VASSILYEVNA STAHOV, whose maiden name was Shubin, had been left an orphan at the age of seven, the heiress to a fairly substantial estate. Her relations on her father's side were very poor, those on her mother's very wealthy; among the latter were Senator Volgin and the Princess Chikurassov. Prince Ardalion Chikurassov, who became her guardian, had her educated in the best Moscow boarding-school, and when she left there he took her into his own home. He entertained freely and gave balls in winter. Her future husband, Nikolai Artyomevich Stahov, had won her hand at one of these balls, an occasion on which she had been wearing 'a charming pink gown with a coiffure of small roses'. She had kept that coiffure.

Nikolai Artyomevich Stahov was the son of a retired captain who had been wounded in 1812 and then had secured a good position in St Petersburg. When Nikolai was sixteen he entered a military school and later passed out into the guards. He was a handsome, well-built young man and was considered to be almost the best dancing partner at the moderately smart parties which he mainly frequented: he had not the entrée to high society. In his youth two dreams had occupied his mind: to get himself promoted aide-de-camp and to marry well. He soon lost the first ambition, but clung all the more persistently to the second; hence he went to Moscow each winter. He spoke French tolerably well, and because he did not lead a dissipated life, had the reputation of being a philosopher.

35

Even when still a subaltern he would argue persistently about such questions as whether it was possible to visit all parts of the world in the course of a lifetime, or to know what went on at the bottom of the sea – and he always maintained that it was not possible.

Stahov was twenty-five years old when he 'landed' Anna Vassilyevna. Then he had retired from the service and gone to live in the country to manage his estate. He soon got bored with living in the country, for his estate was hired out to his peasants who paid him rent instead of service; so he settled in Moscow at his wife's house. In his youth he had not played any sort of game, but now he conceived a passion for lotto, and when that was prohibited, for whist. At home he was bored; he started an affair with a widow of German extraction with whom he spent almost all his time. In the summer of 1853 he did not go to Kuntsovo, but stayed in Moscow – ostensibly to take the waters, but in fact because he did not want to be parted from his widow. However, even with her he had little conversation, but as usual mostly argued about whether you can forecast the weather, and so on. Somebody once called him a sceptic, a *frondeur* – and that pleased him very much. 'Yes,' he thought, self-complacently turning down the corners of his mouth and swaying to and fro, 'I'm not easily satisfied; you can't fool me.' Nikolai Artyomevich's 'frondeurism' consisted in hearing, for example, the word 'nerves' and asking 'What may nerves be' – or if someone referred to the achievements of astronomy, saying: 'So you believe in astronomy.' But when he wanted finally to confound an adversary he would say: 'All that's just words.' To many people, admittedly, this sort of retort seemed – and still does seem – unanswerable; but Nikolai Artyomevich little suspected that Avgustina

36

Christianovna, in letters to her cousin Feodolinda Peterzelius, used to call him 'my simpleton'.

His wife, Anna Vassilyevna, was small and thin, with delicate features, and was given to emotional agitation and melancholy. At school she had studied music and read novels – then had given it all up; she had begun to take an interest in dress, and had given that up too; she had no sooner undertaken the education of her daughter than she had felt it was too much for her and handed the girl over to a governess; and in the end she did nothing but pine and quietly give way to her emotions. The birth of Elena Nikolayevna had upset her health, and she could not have any more children; Nikolai Artyomevich would hint at this fact in justifying his friendship with Avgustina Christianovna. The unfaithfulness of her husband deeply grieved her; it had been particularly mortifying when he surreptitiously gave the German woman a pair of grey horses from her own stud. She never blamed him to his face, but secretly complained about him to everyone in the house in turn, even to her daughter. Anna Vassilyevna did not like going out, but enjoyed it when a visitor came and stayed for a chat; left alone, she at once began to ail. She was an affectionate, tender-hearted woman, and life had quickly crushed her.

Pavel Yakovlevich Shubin was the son of a distant cousin; his father had been in government service in Moscow. Pavel's brothers had entered the corps of cadets but he, the youngest of them and his mother's favourite, was of delicate constitution and had stayed at home. Destined for the university, he had, with difficulty, been maintained at the high school. From his early years he had shown an inclination to sculpture; the portly Senator Volgin, having once seen one of his statuettes at his aunt's house (he was sixteen at the time), had announced that he intended to patronize the talented youth. The sudden death of Shubin's father had almost changed the young man's whole future. The Senator, that patron of talent, presented him with a plaster bust of Homer – and that was all; but Anna Vassilyevna helped him with money, and at the age of nineteen he just managed to enter the university to study medicine. Pavel had not the slightest leaning towards medicine, but with the vacancies for students open at the time it was impossible to enter any other faculty; besides, he was hoping to learn some anatomy. However, he did not learn anatomy; without staying for the second year, or waiting for the examinations, he left the university in order to devote himself wholly to his vocation. He worked intensively, but by fits and starts; he wandered about the outskirts of Moscow drawing and modelling peasant girls, mixing with all and sundry, with young people and old, of high station and low, with Italian moulders and Russian painters; he would not hear of the Art School or acknowledge any master. Talent he had, unquestionably, and he began to be known in Moscow. His mother, a kindly and intelligent woman of good family, and a Parisian by birth, had taken a pride in him, taught him to speak French and tended and fussed over him day and night; but she had died comparatively young of consumption, when Pavel was twenty-one, and had persuaded Anna Vassilyevna to take him under her care. Anna Vassilyevna had fulfilled her last wish; Shubin now occupied a small room in the wing of the villa.

IV

'COME along, come to dinner,' said the mistress of the house in plaintive tones, and all made for the dining-room. 'Sit next to me, Zoya,' Anna Vassilyevna said, 'and Elena, look after the visitor ... And, Pavel, please behave yourself, and don't tease Zoya. My head aches today.'

Again Shubin rolled his eyes upwards: Zoya answered him with a half-smile.

This Zoya, or to speak more accurately, Zoya Nikitishna Mueller, was a nice-looking Russian-German girl, blonde and plump, with a slight cast, a tiny 'dimple' at the tip of her nose, and tiny red lips. She could sing a Russian ballad very decently, and could play a variety of gay and tender pieces on the piano deftly enough; she dressed with taste, but somehow childishly and a little too neatly. Anna Vassilyevna had engaged her as a companion for her daughter, and then had almost always kept her to herself; Elena did not complain of this, for she had no idea what to talk to Zoya about, when they happened to be left alone together.

Dinner lasted for some time; Bersyenev talked to Elena about university life and his hopes and intentions. Shubin listened in silence, ate with exaggerated gusto and occasionally threw a humorously dejected glance at Zoya, who invariably answered him with the same phlegmatic smile. After dinner Elena went out with Bersyenev and Shubin into the garden; Zoya gazed after them, and then, with a slight shrug of the shoulders, sat down at the piano.

'Why don't you go for a walk, too?' Anna Vassilyevna asked – and added, without waiting for an answer, 'Play something to me, something sad . . .'

'*La Dernière Pensée de Weber*?' Zoya asked.

'Oh, yes, Weber,' Anna Vassilyevna said, sinking into an arm-chair; and tears glistened on her eyelashes.

Meanwhile Elena had taken the two friends to an arbour formed of acacia trees; a small table stood in the middle, and there were benches round it. Suddenly Shubin looked back, skipped into the air several times and muttering 'Wait' under his breath, ran back to his room. He returned with a piece of clay and began to model a figure of Zoya, wagging his head, muttering and chuckling as he did so.

'The same old game,' Elena said, glancing at his work; then she turned to Bersyenev to continue the talk they had started at dinner.

'Old game!' Shubin repeated. 'This subject is simply inexhaustible. She tried my patience more than usual today.'

'Why so?' Elena asked. 'Anyone would think you were talking about some nasty, spiteful old woman. A nice-looking young girl . . .'

'Of course,' Shubin interrupted, 'I know she's pretty – very pretty; I'm sure that any passer-by looking at her would be bound to think: "She'd be a fine one to . . . dance the polka with." Also, I'm sure that she knows it and likes it – otherwise, why all these bashful mannerisms, all this modesty? Well, you know what I mean,' he added contemptuously – 'anyway, you're otherwise engaged just now.'

And crushing the figure of Zoya he began, as if in annoyance, rapidly to knead and model the clay.

'So you'd like to be a professor?' Elena asked Bersyenev.

'Yes,' he replied, squeezing his red hands between his knees, 'that's my favourite dream. Of course, I know well enough all the things I lack to make me worthy of such a high . . . I mean, I'm not properly prepared; but I'm hoping to get permission to go abroad. I shall spend three or four years there if need be, and then –'

He stopped, looked down, then raising his eyes quickly, he smiled awkwardly and smoothed his hair. When Bersyenev talked to a woman his speech became still slower, his lisp more noticeable.

'You want to be a professor of history?' Elena asked.

'Yes, or philosophy,' he said, lowering his voice, 'if it is possible.'

'He's devilish strong on philosophy already,' Shubin observed, scoring deep lines in the clay with his finger-nail. 'What does he want to go abroad for?'

'And would you be perfectly contented in that position?' Elena asked, leaning on her elbow and looking him straight in the face.

'Perfectly, Elena Nikolayevna, perfectly. What could be a finer vocation? Just think, to follow in the footsteps of Timofei Nikolayevich!* The very thought of work like that fills me with delight and . . . yes, with a sort of embarrassment, too, due to my awareness of my own deficiencies. My dear father gave me his blessing in the work. I shall never forget his last words.'

'Your father died this last winter?'

'Yes, Elena Nikolayevna, in February.'

'They say,' Elena went on, 'that he left a remarkable work in manuscript – is that true?'

* Timofei Nikolayevich Granovski (1813–55) – Professor of Universal History in Moscow University.

41

'That is so. Oh, he was a wonderful man. You'd have liked him, Elena Nikolayevna.'

'I'm sure of it. And what was this work of his about?'

'That would be rather difficult to explain in a few words, Elena Nikolayevna. My father was a very learned man, a Schellingian, and sometimes he expressed himself rather obscurely.'

'Andrei Petrovich,' Elena interrupted, 'forgive my ignorance, but what does it mean: Schellingian?'

Bersyenev smiled lightly.

'Schellingian means a follower of Schelling, the German philosopher; as to what the doctrine of Schelling consists of –'

'Andrei Petrovich,' Shubin exclaimed, 'for Heaven's sake – surely you're not proposing to give Elena Nikolayevna a lecture on Schelling? Have pity!'

'Not a lecture at all,' Bersyenev muttered and reddened; 'I meant to –'

'And why shouldn't it be a lecture?' Elena put in. 'You and I are much in need of lectures, Pavel Yakovlevich.'

Shubin stared at her and suddenly laughed.

'And what are you laughing for?' she asked coldly, almost sharply.

Shubin was silent.

'All right, all right,' he said, after a pause, 'don't be cross. I'm guilty. But really, I ask you, what a queer taste, to want to talk about philosophy now, in weather like this, under these trees. Better talk about roses and nightingales and youthful eyes and smiles.'

'Yes, and about French novels and women's fashions,' Elena added.

'Why not about women's fashions,' retorted Shubin, 'if they're beautiful.'

'Why not! But suppose we don't want to talk about fashions? You proclaim your freedom as an artist, then why do you interfere with other people's freedom? And may I ask, if these are your views, why you keep going for Zoya? She'd be a particularly suitable person for a discussion about fashions and roses.'

Shubin flared up suddenly, jumping up in his seat.

'So that's it,' he said unsteadily, 'I can take your hint! You're sending me off to her, Elena Nikolayevna! In other words, I'm *de trop* here?'

'I didn't mean to send you away from here.'

'What you mean,' he went on hotly, 'is that I'm not worthy of other society, that I'm just such another as her, that I'm as empty-headed and silly and petty as that sugary German girl? Isn't that it?'

Elena frowned.

'You didn't always talk like that about her, Pavel Yakovlevich,' she observed.

'Aha! A reproach! You're reproaching me now!' Shubin exclaimed. 'Well yes, I don't conceal it, there was a moment, just a moment, when those fresh, commonplace cheeks ... But if I wanted to pay you back in your own coin I might remind you ... Good-bye,' he added suddenly, 'I was going to talk nonsense.'

He gave the clay, which he had modelled into the shape of a head, a slap with his hand, ran out of the arbour and went back to his room.

'What a child,' Elena said, looking after him.

'An artist,' observed Bersyenev with a quiet smile. 'All artists are like that. You have to forgive their tantrums. That's their right.'

'Yes,' Elena retorted, '– but up to the present Pavel hasn't established any such right. What has he done up to

43

now? Give me your arm and let us walk up the avenue. He interrupted us. We were talking about your father's work.'

Bersyenev took Elena's arm and they walked together in the garden; but the conversation which had been prematurely cut short was not resumed. Bersyenev began once more to expound his view of the professor's calling and of his own future activities. He walked slowly at her side, with awkward gait, awkwardly holding her arm, occasionally touching her with his shoulder and never once looking at her; but his words flowed easily, if not with complete freedom; he spoke simply and sincerely and his eyes, roving slowly over the tree-trunks and the gravel path and the grass, shone with the quiet emotion which fine sentiments inspire; in his voice, which was calmer now, could be discerned the joy of a man who knew that he was successfully expressing himself to someone dear to him. Elena listened to him attentively; half turning towards him, she fixed her gaze on his face, which had paled a little, and on his eyes, which were gentle and friendly, though they avoided meeting her own. Her soul was opened up and it seemed that something tender, just and good was flowing into her heart, or growing up in it.

V

SHUBIN had not left his room when night fell. It was already quite dark, the waxing moon was high in the sky, the Milky Way shone white and the stars were twinkling, when Bersyenev, having taken leave of Anna Vassilyevna, Elena and Zoya, approached the door of his friend's room. He found it bolted, and knocked.

'Who's there?' Shubin's voice rang out.

'I,' answered Bersyenev.

'What do you want?'

'Let me in, Pavel, and do stop sulking; aren't you ashamed of yourself?'

'I'm not sulking, I'm asleep and dreaming of Zoya.'

'Stop it, please. You're not a baby. Let me in. I must talk to you.'

'Haven't you talked yourself out with Elena?'

'That's enough of it, Pavel; let me in!'

Shubin's answer was an affected snore; Bersyenev shrugged his shoulders and set off home.

The night was warm and somehow exceptionally silent; it was if everything around was listening and watching, and Bersyenev, gripped by the still darkness, stopped involuntarily and likewise listened and watched. A faint sound like the rustle of a woman's dress started up intermittently in the tops of the near-by trees, and aroused in Bersyenev a sensation of sweetness, of mystery, almost of fear; his skin tingled, his eyes were chilled with momentary tears; he felt he wanted to tread quite silently, to walk

45

on tip-toe, to conceal himself; a keen wind blew from the side and made him shudder slightly and stop dead; a sleepy beetle fell from a branch and bumped on the road – he cried 'Oh' softly, and stopped again. But he began to think of Elena and all these fleeting impressions vanished at once: there remained only the invigorating sense of the night's freshness, of the night's walk; his whole being was filled with the young girl's image. Bersyenev was walking with his head bowed, recalling her words, her questions . . . He thought he heard the tramp of hurried steps behind him. He listened . . . someone was running, someone was overtaking him – he heard gasps of breath – and suddenly, out of the black circle of shadow cast by a large tree, hatless, his hair dishevelled, all pale in the light of the moon, Shubin emerged before him.

'I'm glad you went this way,' he said, with difficulty, 'I shouldn't have slept all night, if I hadn't caught you. Let me take your arm. You're going home, aren't you?'

'Yes.'

'I'll come with you.'

'But how can you go without a hat? . . .'

'It's nothing. I took my tie off too. It's warm to-night.'

The friends walked on a few paces.

'I was very stupid today, wasn't I?' Shubin asked suddenly.

'Frankly, yes. I couldn't understand you. I've never seen you like that. And what on earth were you angry about? What trifling thing?'

'Hm,' Shubin growled, 'that's what you say, but for me it's no trifling matter. You see,' he added, 'I must tell you that I . . . that . . . you can think what you like about me, but – you see, I'm in love with Elena.'

'You in love with Elena!' Bersyenev repeated and stood still.

'Yes,' Shubin continued in a tone of forced indifference, 'does that surprise you? I'll tell you something else. Up to this evening I might have hoped that with time she would come to love me too. But today convinced me that I've nothing to hope for. She has come to love – someone else.'

'Someone else? But who?'

'Who? You!' Shubin cried, and slapped Bersyenev on the shoulder.

'Me!'

'You,' Shubin repeated.

Bersyenev fell back a pace and stood motionless. Shubin looked at him keenly.

'Does that surprise you too? You're a modest young man. But she does love you. You can rest assured of that.'

'What nonsense you're talking,' Bersyenev said at length, with annoyance.

'No, it's not nonsense. What are we stopping for, anyway? Let's go on, it's easier walking. I've known her a long time, and I know her well: I can't be mistaken. She's taken a fancy to you. There was a time when she liked me; but in the first place I'm too frivolous a young man for her, whereas you're a serious creature, morally and physically a decent personality, you – no, I've not finished yet – you're a visionary, but a scrupulously moderate visionary, a true representative of that scientific priesthood of which – no, not of which – on account of which the middle strata of the Russian aristocracy are so justly proud! ... And secondly, the other day Elena caught me kissing Zoya's arms!'

'Zoya's?'

'Yes, Zoya's. What do you expect? . . . She's got such nice shoulders.'

'Shoulders?'

'Well, shoulders, arms, isn't it all the same? Elena caught me after dinner behaving in this rather free and easy way, and before dinner I'd been abusing Zoya in her presence. Unfortunately Elena doesn't understand the perfect naturalness of such contradictions. At this point you turned up; you're a man who believes in – now what do you believe in? – you blush, you get embarrassed, you agonize about Schiller and Schelling (she's always on the look-out for remarkable men) and so it is you win – while I, poor unfortunate one, try to make jokes and . . . in the meantime . . .'

Shubin suddenly began to weep and, walking to one side, he sat down on the ground grasping his hair.

Bersyenev went up to him.

'Pavel,' he began, 'what childishness this is. Now, really – what's come over you today? God knows what nonsense has got into your head, you're actually crying. Honestly, it seems to me that you're putting it on.'

Shubin raised his head: tears were glistening on his cheeks in the moonlight, but his face was smiling.

'Andrei Petrovich,' he said, 'you can think what you like of me. I'm even prepared to admit that I'm a bit hysterical just now – but it's God's truth that I'm in love with Elena and that Elena loves you! However, I promised to see you home, and I'll keep my promise.'

He got up.

'What a night! How silvery, dark and young! How grand it must be now if you know that someone loves you – what a joy not to get to sleep! Will you sleep, Andrei Petrovich?'

Bersyenev did not answer, but walked faster.

'Where are you hurrying to?' Shubin continued. 'Believe me, there won't be another night like this one in all your life – but at home, Schelling awaits you. It's true he served you in good stead today, but all the same don't be in such a hurry; you should be singing, if you know how to, you should be singing aloud; and if you can't, then take off your hat and throw back your head and smile at the stars. They're all watching you, only you; that's all the stars do, look at lovers – that's why they're so beautiful. You are in love, Andrei, aren't you? You don't answer – why don't you answer?' Shubin started again. 'Oh, keep silent then, if you feel happy, keep silent! I'm jabbering away like this because I'm a poor devil that nobody loves, an actor, a conjurer, a clown – but what draughts of unspeakable joy I'd be drinking out in this night air, under these stars, under these jewels of stars – if only I knew that someone loved me! Bersyenev, are you happy?'

Bersyenev remained silent as before, and walked quickly along the level road. Among the trees in front glimmered the lights of the little village where he lived: it consisted only of ten small cottages. Just where the village began, to the right of the road, under two spreading birch trees, there was a small shop. The windows were already closed, but a broad band of light struck fanlike from the open door on to the trodden grass and up through the trees, sharply illuminating the greenish-white undersides of the densely growing leaves. A girl who looked like a servant was standing in the shop with her back to the door, bargaining with the shopkeeper. Her chubby cheeks and slender neck were scarcely visible under the red shawl which she had thrown over her head and was holding to her chin with her bare hand. The young men stepped into the beam of light . . .

Shubin glanced into the shop, stopped and called out: 'Annushka!' The girl turned round quickly, disclosing a pretty, rather broad face, with a fresh complexion, cheerful brown eyes and black eyebrows. 'Annushka,' Shubin repeated. The girl peered at him, startled and confused – then, without finishing her shopping, ran down the steps, slipped quickly past them and glancing over her shoulder, crossed over the road to the left. The shopkeeper, a fat and quite imperturbable person, like all country tradesmen, grunted and yawned after her, while Shubin turned to Bersyenev and said: 'That was – you see, that was – there's a family here that I know – and that was their – you mustn't think –' and without finishing he ran off after the retreating girl.

'At least wipe away your tears,' Bersyenev called to him, and could not help laughing. But when he got home the gaiety had gone from his face, he was no longer laughing. He did not for a moment believe what Shubin had told him, but his words had made a deep impression on him. 'Pavel was fooling me,' he thought, 'but some day she will love someone . . . Who will that be?'

In Bersyenev's room there was a piano, small and old, but with a soft and pleasant tone, though it was not quite in tune. Bersyenev sat down at it and began to strum out some chords. Like every Russian of gentle birth he had been taught music in his youth, and like most such people he played very badly; but he loved music passionately. Properly speaking it was not the art of musical expression that he loved, not the form (symphonies and sonatas, even operas made him feel dejected), but the basic elements: he loved the vague, sweet, aimless, all-embracing feelings which combinations and modulations of sound roused in his heart. For more than an hour he stayed at the piano, repeating the same chords over and over again, clumsily seeking for new ones, pausing entranced over minor sevenths. His heart ached and more than once his eyes filled with tears; he was not ashamed of them, for they were shed in darkness. 'Pavel is right,' he thought, 'I can feel it now: this evening will never be repeated.' At last he rose, lit a candle, put on a dressing-gown, and fetched the second volume of Raumer's *History of the Hohenstaufen* from the shelf – then, sighing once or twice, he settled down to read.

VI

MEANWHILE Elena returned to her room, sat down in front of the open window and leaned her head on her hand. It had become a habit with her to spend about a quarter of an hour each evening by the window of her room. On these occasions she would talk things over in her own mind, and give herself an account of the past day. Not long past her twentieth birthday, she was a tall girl, with a dark pallid complexion, and her large grey eyes, under arched eyebrows, were flecked round with tiny freckles; her forehead and nose were quite straight, her mouth was firmly closed, her chin rather pointed; her light brown hair grew low on her slim neck. In everything about her, in the alert and rather nervous expression of her face, in her clear but changeable eyes, in her strained-looking smile and quiet uneven voice there was something tense and electric, something impulsive and hasty, something, in a word, which not everyone could like, and which to some people was even repellent. Her pink hands were slender, with long fingers; her feet were slender also. She walked quickly, almost impetuously, leaning forward slightly. Her emotional development had been strange; at first she had adored her father, then she had become passionately attached to her mother, and then had cooled towards both of them, especially to her father. Recently she had treated her mother as if she were an ailing grandmother; while her father, who had been proud of her as long as she had the reputation of being an unusual child, began to be afraid of her when she grew up, and spoke of her as a sort of enraptured republican girl – 'God knew whom she took after.' Weakness of character made her indignant, stupidity angered her, a lie she would not forgive 'as long as she lived'. Nothing would make her give way in her demands, even her prayers were often mixed with reproaches. A person had but to lose her respect – and she passed judgement quickly, often too quickly – and at once he ceased to exist for her. Every impression was imprinted sharply on her soul; life, for her, was no light matter.

The governess to whom Anna Vassilyevna had confided the completion of her daughter's education – an education, by the way, which the dispirited mother had not even started – was of Russian stock, a girl from a young ladies' academy, and the daughter of a man who had taken bribes and come to ruin; she was a very sentimental, kind and untruthful creature. After repeatedly falling in love she had finished by marrying an officer of sorts who promptly abandoned her; that was in 1850, when Elena was seventeen. This governess was very fond of literature and herself wrote little verses; she inspired in her pupil a love of reading, but reading alone would not satisfy Elena. From her childhood she had longed for action, for active goodness; the poor, the hungry and the sick concerned her, worried her, tortured her. She dreamt of them, and cross-questioned all her acquaintances about them. She gave her alms with careful thought, with an instinctive gravity, almost with emotion. Every down-trodden animal, every underfed dog, kittens condemned to death, sparrows fallen from the nest, even insects and reptiles, found in Elena succour and protection; she fed them herself and was never put off by their wretchedness. Her mother did not interfere, but her father was most indignant about her –

about what he called her vulgar tender-heartedness – and declared that it was impossible to move about the house for dogs and cats. 'Lenochka,' he would call out to her, 'come quickly, there's a spider eating a fly, you must set the poor thing free' – and Lenochka, thoroughly alarmed, would come running up, free the fly and unstick its legs. 'And now let it bite you if you're so kind-hearted,' her father would say ironically; but she did not listen. When she was ten she got to know a beggar-girl called Katya; she used to go secretly and meet her in the garden and take her sweets and cakes, and give her presents of scarves and sixpences – Katya wouldn't take toys. They used to sit side by side on the ground among the shrubs behind some nettles, and Elena with a joyous feeling of humility would eat Katya's stale bread and listen to her stories. Katya had a wicked old aunt who often used to beat her; Katya hated her and was always saying how she would run away from her aunt and live 'in God's free world'; with a sense of secret respect and awe Elena listened to these strange novel ideas, watching her fixedly, and at the time everything about her, the sharp, black, almost animal-like eyes, the sunburnt hands and husky voice, even the ragged dress, seemed somehow to take on a special, almost a holy character. Elena would return to the house and for a long time afterwards think about the poor and about 'God's free world'; she thought how she would cut herself a hazel stick and take a beggar's bag and run away with Katya and wander along the highways with a garland of cornflowers on her head; once she had seen Katya with a garland like that. If any of her family happened to come into the room then, she would turn shy and look sullen. Once she had run off to meet Katya in the rain, and got her dress dirty; her father saw her and called her a dirty peasant girl. She flushed all over – and a marvellous frightening feeling came over her. Katya often used to sing a wild soldiers' ditty, and Elena learnt it from her . . . Anna Vassilyevna happened to overhear it and was outraged.

'Where did you pick up that horrible stuff?' she asked her daughter.

Elena merely looked at her mother and said nothing; she felt she would rather let them tear her to pieces than give away her secret; and again that sweet, fearful sensation came upon her. However, her friendship with Katya did not last long; the poor girl fell ill of a fever, and died after a few days.

Elena grieved bitterly when she heard of the death of Katya, and for a long time could not get to sleep at nights; the last words of the beggar-girl rang ceaselessly in her ears, and they seemed to be calling her . . .

And so the years slipped by – quickly and imperceptibly, like water under the snow. Elena's childhood flowed away, outwardly in idleness, inwardly in conflict and turmoil. Friends she had none; of all the girls who visited the Stahovs' house she did not get to know one well. Parental authority never weighed heavily on Elena, and from her sixteenth year she had become almost entirely independent. She led her own life, but a lonely life. In solitude her soul would blaze up and subside; she struggled like a bird in a cage, though there was no cage; no one restricted or re-strained her – yet she struggled, and languished.

Sometimes she could not understand herself – she even feared herself. Everything around her seemed meaningless or incomprehensible. 'What is life without love?' she thought, 'but there's no one to love!' and such thoughts, such feelings began to alarm her. When she was eighteen she almost died of a fever. Her constitution, strong and

55

healthy by nature, was seriously shaken, and for a long time could not right itself. At length the last traces of the disease passed away, but Elena's father continued to talk resentfully of her nerves. Sometimes it seemed to her that she wanted something that no one else wanted, that no one dreamed of in all Russia. Then she would calm down, and spend day after day in carefree indifference, even laughing at herself; but suddenly some strong, some nameless thing which she could not control boiled up inside her and demanded to break out. The storm passed, the tired wings dropped without having flown; but these moods were not without their cost; however much she tried not to disclose what was going on inside her, her very tranquillity betrayed the anguish of her turbulent spirit, and her parents often and with reason shrugged their shoulders in astonishment, unable to understand her 'strangeness'.

On the day when our story begins, Elena stayed longer than usual at the window. She thought a great deal about Bersyenev and about her talk with him. She liked him, and had faith in the warmth of his feelings and the sincerity of his intentions. He had never before spoken to her as he had done that evening. She recalled the expression of his diffident eyes, of his smile – and she herself fell to smiling and musing, though her thoughts were no longer of him. She gazed into the night through the open window. For a long time she looked into the dark low-hanging sky; then she stood up, flicked her hair from her face with a movement of her head and – without herself knowing why – stretched out her bare cool arms to the sky, that sky; then she let them fall, and knelt down by her bed; she pressed her face to the pillow, and in spite of all her efforts not to give way to the feelings which were flooding over her she began to weep strange, bewildered, burning tears.

VII

THE next day soon after eleven Bersyenev set off for Moscow in a returning cab. He had to get some money from the post office and buy some books, and in addition he wanted to call and see Insarov. When he had last been talking to Shubin, the idea had occurred to him that he might invite Insarov down to stay with him in the country. It was some time before he found him. He had moved from his former lodging and the new one was not easy to locate: it was in the courtyard at the back of an ugly brick house built in the Petersburg style between the Arbat and Povarkaya streets. In vain Bersyenev wandered from one dirty flight of steps to another, in vain he called for a porter or anyone else who would listen. Even in St Petersburg porters avoid the eye of a visitor, and in Moscow this habit is still more widespread: no one answered Bersyenev; only an inquisitive tailor in his shirt-sleeves, with a skein of grey thread over his shoulder and a black eye, silently stuck his grubby unshaven face out of a high casement window, and a black hornless goat, which had climbed on to the top of a dung-heap, turned round and bleated plaintively and began to chew its cud more vigorously than before. At last a woman in an old coat and down-at-heel shoes took pity on him, and showed him where Insarov's lodging was. Bersyenev found him at home. He had rented a room from the tailor – the same that had observed, with such indifference, Bersyenev's perplexed wanderings. It was a big, almost completely empty room, with dark green walls, three square windows, a tiny bed in one corner and a small leather sofa in another, and hanging just below the ceiling was an enormous cage, in which at one time there had been a nightingale. As soon as Bersyenev crossed the threshold, Insarov came to meet him; he did not greet him with: 'Why, it's you!' or: 'Good heavens, what's brought you here?' or even: 'How are you?' but simply pressed his hand and led him to the only chair in the room.

'Sit down,' he said, as he himself sat on the edge of the table. 'You see, I'm still in a muddle,' he added, pointing to the heap of papers and books on the floor: 'I've not got myself properly installed yet; I haven't had time.'

Insarov spoke Russian perfectly correctly, pronouncing each word clearly and forcibly; but his guttural, though agreeable voice was somehow not Russian. Insarov's foreign origin – he was a Bulgarian by birth – showed itself still more obviously in his appearance: he was a young man of about twenty-five, lean and sinewy, with straight blue-black hair, a hollow chest and bony hands. He had sharp features, an aquiline nose, a smallish forehead, small, steady, deep-set eyes and thick eyebrows; when he smiled his fine white teeth showed momentarily from behind his thin, hard, over-precise lips. He was wearing an old but neat jacket, buttoned up to the neck.

'Why did you move from your last lodgings?' Bersyenev asked him.

'This is cheaper: nearer the university.'

'But it's vacation-time now . . . and fancy wanting to live in town in the summer! You might as well have taken a cottage, once you'd decided to move.'

Insarov did not answer – and offering Bersyenev a pipe observed: 'Forgive me, I don't possess cigarettes or cigars.'

Bersyenev lit the pipe.

'Now I,' he continued, 'I've taken a cottage down near Kuntsovo – very cheap and very comfortable. In fact there's even a spare room upstairs.'

Again Insarov did not answer. Bersyenev sucked at his pipe.

'I even thought,' he began again, blowing out thin whiffs of smoke, 'that perhaps there was anyone – you, for instance – who would like – who would be willing to lodge down there with me, in the upstairs room – how nice it would be! What do you think, Dmitri Nikanorovich?'

Insarov looked up with his small eyes.

'You're suggesting I should live with you in the country?'

'Yes: I've a spare room upstairs.'

'I'm very grateful to you Andrei Petrovich, but I don't feel my means permit it.'

'How do you mean, don't permit it?'

'They don't permit me to live in the country. I can't keep two lodgings.'

'But you know I . . .' Bersyenev was beginning and then stopped. 'It wouldn't mean any extra expense,' he went on. 'Let's suppose you keep on your room here: against that, everything down there is very cheap. We might even arrange it, perhaps, so that we could have meals together.'

Insarov was silent. Bersyenev felt awkward.

'At least visit me sometime,' he began, after a pause; 'just a step from where I live there's a family I'd very much like you to know. There's a marvellous girl there, Insarov, if you only knew! One of my best friends lives there too, a man of great talent – I'm sure you'd get on with him.' (Russians love to be generous – if with nothing else, with their own friends.) 'Really, you must come. And better still, come and stay with us – yes, do. We could work and read together: you know I'm studying history and philosophy. It's all of interest to you, and I have plenty of books.'

Insarov got up and walked about the room.

'Excuse my asking,' he said at last; 'how much do you pay for your cottage?'

'A hundred roubles.'

'And how many rooms are there?'

'Five.'

'So at that rate one room would cost twenty roubles?'

'At that rate . . . now, really, I don't need the room at all. It's simply empty.'

'Possibly; but listen,' Insarov went on, with a determined and at the same time frank and unaffected shake of the head, 'I could only take advantage of your offer if you agreed to accept a fair share of the rent. I'm in a position to pay twenty roubles – the more so as I shall be able to economize on all the other things, according to what you say.'

'Of course: but really, I shall feel conscience-stricken about it.'

'I couldn't do it otherwise, Andrei Petrovich.'

'Well, as you wish – but how obstinate you are!'

Insarov again said nothing.

The young men agreed which day Insarov should move. They called for the landlord, but he first sent his daughter, a girl of about seven, with an enormous patterned shawl on her head. She listened attentively, almost with terror, to everything Insarov told her, and then disappeared in silence. After her, the mother appeared – a woman far gone with child – who also wore a shawl on her head, but only a tiny one. Insarov explained that he was going to move to a cottage near Kuntsovo, but that he was keeping his room and leaving his things in her care; the tailor's wife also seemed frightened, and went away. At last the landlord himself came; at first he seemed to understand everything that was said and merely observed thoughtfully, 'Near Kuntsovo?' – but then he suddenly unlatched the door and shouted: 'Are you going to keep the room then?' Insarov calmed him down. 'Because it's necessary to know,' repeated the tailor sternly, and disappeared.

Bersyenev set off home, well satisfied with the success of his plan. Insarov, with a friendly civility little seen in Russia, accompanied him to the door; left alone, he carefully took off his jacket and began to go through his papers.

VIII

On the evening of the same day Anna Vassilyevna was
sitting in her drawing-room on the brink of tears. With her
in the room was her husband and also a distant uncle of his,
Uvar Ivanovich Stahov, who was a retired cavalry lieutenant of some sixty years of age. He was a man corpulent
to the point of immobility, with small, sleepy, yellow eyes
and thick colourless lips in a bloated yellow face. From the
day of his retirement he had lived continuously in Moscow
on the income from a small inheritance left to him by his
wife, who had been the daughter of a merchant. He did
nothing and hardly even thought; but if he did think, he
kept his thoughts to himself. Only once in his life had he
got excited and shown any particular activity – that was
when he had read in the paper about a new 'anti-bombard-
ment' device on view at the International Exhibition in
London: he wanted to order one for himself, and actually
inquired where he should send the money, and through
what agency. Uvar Ivanovich wore a full-fitting frock coat
of tobacco colour and a white neckcloth; he ate frequently
and much; in moments of embarrassment, which occurred
whenever he had to produce some opinion, he merely
wagged the fingers of his right hand spasmodically, first
from his thumb to his little finger and then from his little
finger to his thumb and uttered with an effort: 'Really ...
I mean to say ... in a way ...'

Uvar Ivanovich sat in an arm-chair by the window
breathing with difficulty, while Nikolai Artyomevich strode

about the room with his hands in his pockets; his face expressed dissatisfaction.

At last he stopped and shook his head.

'Yes,' he began, 'in our day young people were brought up differently: they didn't allow themselves to be undutiful to their elders. But nowadays – well, I merely look on and wonder. Maybe I'm wrong, and they're right; maybe. But all the same, I see things in my own way – and I wasn't born a fool. What's your view of it, Uvar Ivanovich?'

Uvar Ivanovich only looked at him and waggled his fingers.

'Take Elena Nikolayevna, for instance,' Nikolai Artyomevich continued – 'I simply don't understand her. I'm just not up to her level. Her heart is so big it seems to embrace all nature – down to the merest frog or cockroach – in fact, everything except her own father. Very well, I know it and I leave her alone. You see she's highly strung, a blue-stocking, up in the clouds – and all that's not in my line. But this Mr Shubin – let's admit he's a wonderful, an extraordinary artist, I'll not dispute that – but to be disrespectful to an older man, a man, when all's said and done, to whom he owes a great deal – well, I confess, *dans mon gros bon sens*, I can't stand for that! I don't ask much, that's my nature, but there's a limit to everything.'

Anna Vassilyevna rang the bell in great agitation, and a boy entered.

'How is it Pavel Yakovlevich doesn't come?' she said. 'Why doesn't he come when I call?'

Nikolai Artyomevich shrugged his shoulders. 'Now, really, what do you want to call him for? It's not in the least necessary, in fact I don't want it.'

'What for, Nikolai Artyomevich? He's worried you; he may have upset your course of treatment. I want to have it out with him; I want to know what he did to annoy you.'

'I repeat, it's not necessary. And need you really go on like this – *devant les domestiques*.'

Anna Vassilyevna reddened slightly.

'You shouldn't say that, Nikolai Artyomevich. I never ... *devant les domestiques*. Go along, Fedushka, and mind you bring back Pavel Yakovlevich immediately.'

The boy went out.

'It's not in the least bit necessary,' Nikolai Artyomevich muttered through his teeth, and again began to pace about the room. 'I never meant to suggest it.'

'But surely Pavel ought to apologize to you.'

'But what use are his apologies to me? What's an apology, anyway? All that's just words.'

'What use are they? He must be taught to see reason.'

'You teach him yourself. He'd sooner listen to you. And I've no grievance against him.'

'No, Nikolai Artyomevich, you've been out of humour ever since you arrived today. I can see with my own eyes you've lost weight recently. I'm afraid your treatment isn't doing you good.'

'The treatment's essential,' Nikolai Artyomevich observed; 'my liver's out of order.'

At this moment Shubin entered. A faint, slightly sarcastic smile was on his lips.

'Did you send for me, Anna Vassilyevna?' he said.

'Yes, of course I sent for you. Really, Pavel, this is terrible. I'm most dissatisfied with you. How could you show disrespect for Nikolai Artyomevich?'

'Has Nikolai Artyomevich been complaining about

64

me?' Shubin asked, looking at Stahov with the sneer still on his lips.

Stahov turned away and looked down.

'Yes, he has been complaining. I don't know what you did to injure him, but you must apologize at once, because he's not at all well just now, and anyway young people should always show respect to people who have helped them.'

'Oh, the logic!' Shubin thought and turned to Stahov.

'I'm ready to apologize to you, Nikolai Artyomevich,' he said, making a polite little bow, 'if I've offended you in any way at all.'

'Not at all – it isn't that,' Nikolai Artyomevich retorted, still avoiding Shubin's eyes. 'However, I'm glad to forgive you – you know I'm an easygoing sort of person.'

'Oh, I'm sure of it, no one could doubt it!' Shubin observed. 'But forgive my curiosity: does Anna Vassilyevna actually know what I did wrong?'

'No, I don't know anything,' Anna Vassilyevna remarked, stretching her head forward as if to hear what was coming.

'Oh, my God!' Nikolai Artyomevich exclaimed, and went on quickly, 'How many times have I begged and entreated . . . how many times have I said how disgusting I find these scenes and explanations! You come home once in a blue moon and you want to relax – people talk about the family circle, *l'intérieur*, and being a family man – but here you just have scenes and unpleasantness. There's not a minute's peace. You have to go off to the club or – or somewhere. A man's human, he has a physical being, with its own needs, but here . . .'

And without finishing his speech he went out and banged the door. Anna Vassilyevna watched him go.

'To the club?' she muttered bitterly. 'You aren't going to the club, you feather-head! There's no one at the club to give horses to out of my stable – and grey ones too – my favourite colour. No, you silly man,' she added, raising her voice, 'you aren't going to the club. But you, Pavel,' she went on, getting up, 'aren't you ashamed of yourself? After all, you're not a child. And now my head's started to ache. Where is Zoya, do you know?'

'Upstairs in her room, I think. That clever little fox always hides in her burrow in weather like this!'

'Now please, please!' Anna Vassilyevna looked round for something. 'Have you seen my glass with the grated horse-radish? Pavel, do me a kindness and don't vex me in future.'

'How could I vex you, Aunty dear? Let me kiss your hand. As for your horse-radish, I saw it in the study on the little table.'

'Darya's always leaving it somewhere,' Anna Vassilyevna observed, and went out with a rustle of her silk dress.

Shubin was about to follow her, when he heard the slow voice of Uvar Ivanovich behind him, and stopped.

'You young puppy – he should have given you – something,' the retired lieutenant said haltingly.

Shubin approached him.

'And why should he have given me something, worthy Uvar Ivanovich?'

'Why? You're young – you should show respect.'

'Who for?'

'Who for? You know who for. You may grin.'

Shubin crossed his arms on his chest.

'Oh you – you spokesman of the primitive chorus,' he cried, 'you spirit of the black earth, you foundation of the social edifice!'

Uvar Ivanovich waggled his fingers.

'Enough of it, fellow, don't try me.'

'Now listen,' Shubin continued. 'You're not exactly a youngster, are you, and yet what a world of childlike, happy faith is hidden in your heart! Show respect! And do you know, you primitive creature, what's made Nikolai Artyomevich angry with me? Well then, I spent the whole of this morning with him round at his German woman's; and we were singing a trio together – that thing 'Do Not Leave Me'. You should have heard us, it would have moved you, I think. Well, my dear sir, we sang and we sang – and then I got bored; I could see something was in the air, there was so much tenderness flying about. So I began to tease them both. It worked well. First she got cross with me, then with him; then he got cross with her, and told her he was only happy at home, and *that* was where his Paradise was; she told him that he was immoral, and I said: "Ach!" to her in German; he went away, and I stayed on. He came down here, that is, he came to Paradise, but Paradise makes him sick. So then he falls to grumbling. Now, sir, who's to blame, in your view?'

'You, of course,' Uvar Ivanovich retorted.

Shubin stared at him.

'May I ask you, honourable knight,' he began in mock humility, 'whether you felt impelled to utter those cryptic words as a result of some effort of your cogitative faculties, or were they inspired by a momentary desire on your part to produce the atmospheric disturbance known as sound?'

'Don't try me, I say,' groaned Uvar Ivanovich.

Shubin broke into laughter and ran from the room.

'Hi!' Uvar Ivanovich called out, after a quarter of an hour had passed. 'I say ... a glass of vodka!'

The boy brought vodka and *hors-d'œuvres* on a tray.

Uvar Ivanovich slowly took the glass off the tray, and for a long time gazed at it with strained attention as if he could not clearly make out what was in his hand. He looked at the boy and asked: 'Are you called Vaska?' Then with a pained expression he drank the vodka, ate a snack and stuck his hand in his pocket for a handkerchief . . . Long after the boy had put away the tray and the decanter, and eaten up the remains of the salted herring, and fallen asleep against his master's overcoat, Uvar Ivanovich was still holding the handkerchief before him on his outspread fingers, and gazing with that same strained attention at the window, the floor and the walls.

IX

SHUBIN returned to his room and was just opening a book when Nikolai Artyomevich's valet cautiously entered and handed him a note; it was folded three-cornerwise and heavily sealed with a coat-of-arms. 'I hope' – so the note ran – 'that you, as an honourable man, will not permit yourself to allude with so much as a single word to a certain promissory note which was the subject of discussion this morning; you know my principles and my position in the matter, you know the insignificance of the actual amount and other circumstances; moreover, there are family secrets which must be respected, while family harmony is so sacred that only *êtres sans cœur* – among whom I have no reason to number you – would disregard it. (Return this note) – N. S.'

Shubin wrote underneath in pencil: 'Don't worry – I don't go picking people's pockets yet,' returned the note to the valet, and again took up his book; but it soon slipped out of his hand. He looked out at the reddening sky, and at two sturdy young pine trees which stood apart from the rest: 'During the day,' he thought, 'the pines are a bluish colour, but in the evening how magnificently green they are!' and he went out into the garden, secretly hoping to meet Elena there. He was not disappointed. On the path between the shrubs ahead of him he caught a glimpse of her dress. He went after her and, drawing abreast, said:

'Don't look at me, I'm not worth it.'

She glanced at him quickly, smiled fleetingly, and walked on into the garden. Shubin followed her.

'I ask you not to look at me,' he said, 'and yet I start talking to you; obviously a plain contradiction! However, that's nothing; it's not the first time with me. I've just remembered that I never begged your pardon, as I should have done, for the stupid way I behaved yesterday. You're not angry with me, Elena Nikolayevna?'

She stopped, and at first did not answer him – not because she was angry, but because her thoughts were far away.

Shubin bit his lip.

'How preoccupied your face is – and how indifferent!' he muttered. 'Elena Nikolayevna,' he went on, raising his voice, 'let me tell you a little story about a friend of mine. He too had a friend, a man who always behaved himself respectably until he took to drink. Then one day early in the morning my friend met him in the street (they had already broken off their friendship) and he saw that he was drunk. My friend turned away from him deliberately. But the drunkard came up to him and said: "I would not have minded if you had not greeted me, but why do you turn away? It may be that grief has brought me to this. Peace to my ashes!"'

Shubin was silent.

'And is that all?' Elena asked.

'That is all.'

'I don't understand you. What is it you are suggesting? Just now you said I was not to look at you . . .'

'Yes, and now I have told you how wrong it is to turn away.'

'But did I . . .' Elena was beginning.

'Didn't you?'

70

Elena coloured slightly and stretched out her hand to Shubin. He pressed it warmly.

'It does look as if you'd caught me feeling rather unfriendly towards you,' Elena said; 'but your suspicion is not just. I didn't even think of avoiding you.'

'Granted; granted. But you must admit that at this very minute you've a thousand thoughts in your head, and you're not confiding one of them to me. Well? Isn't it true what I say?'

'Maybe.'

'Then why is it? Why?'

'I'm not clear about my own thoughts.'

'Then now's just the time to tell them to someone else,' Shubin caught her up. 'But I'll tell you what the trouble is; you've a low opinion of me.'

'I?'

'Yes, you. You imagine that everything about me is half-affectation, because I'm an artist; you think that I'm not only incapable of doing anything – you're probably right there – but also of having any genuine, deep feeling, that I can't even weep sincerely, that I talk too much and too maliciously – and all because I'm an artist. What sort of miserable, God-forsaken creatures do you think we are then? I'll swear you don't believe I'm really repentant, for instance.'

'No, Pavel Yakovlevich, I believe in your repentance, and I believe in your tears; but it seems to me that you find even your repentance entertaining – yes, and your tears also.'

Shubin started.

'Oh well, I can see that it's an incurable case, as the doctors say, a *casus incurabilis*. So it only remains to hang my head and submit. Anyhow, my God! how can I go on

71

worrying about my own soul with such a being existing at my side? And to think that I shall never penetrate that being, and never know why she is sad, why she is joyous, what turmoil is going on inside her, where she is going . . . Tell me,' he said, after a short silence, 'could you never, never on any account, never in any circumstances, love an artist?'

Elena looked him straight in the eyes.

'I don't think so, Pavel Yakovlevich; no.'

'Q.E.D.,' said Shubin, with melancholy humour. 'I think, after that, it would be more becoming for me not to interrupt your solitary walk. The professor might have asked you: "On what data do you base this answer: No?" But I'm not a professor; according to your ideas I'm a child; only remember, people don't turn away from children. Good-bye – Peace to my ashes.'

Elena was going to stop him, but after a moment's thought she also said: 'Good-bye.'

Shubin went out of the courtyard. At a short distance from the Stahovs' villa he met Bersyenev. He was walking rapidly, his head bowed and his hat pushed right back on to his neck.

'Andrei Petrovich!' Shubin cried.

Bersyenev stopped.

'Go, go on,' Shubin went on, 'I was only calling you, not stopping you – just slip into the garden, you'll find Elena there. I think she's waiting for you . . . anyway, she's waiting for someone. Do you understand the force of those words: she's waiting? . . . But do you know, my friend, here's rather a surprising thing? Just imagine, here I've been living in the same house with her for two years, and I'm in love with her, too, and yet only now, this very minute – no, I didn't understand her – but I *saw* her. I saw her and I was amazed. Please don't look at me with that psuedo-sarcastic grin, it doesn't suit your sedate features. Oh, yes, I know, you're going to remind me of Annushka. Well, what about it? I don't deny it. Annushka is just the stuff for the likes of us. Three cheers for Annushka and Zoya, I say, yes, and for Avgustina Christianovna, too. Now just you go and see Elena and I'll get along to – to Annushka, you're thinking? No, my friend, worse than that: I'm going to Prince Chikurassov. He's a patron of the arts, a Tartar from Kazan, like Volgin. Just look at this invitation, do you see those letters: R.S.V.P.? Even in the country there's no peace for me! *Addio.*'

Bersyenev listened to Shubin's tirade in silence, and seemed to be a little embarrassed on his account; then he went into the courtyard of the villa. Meanwhile Shubin did in fact go to see Prince Chikurassov, to whom he proceeded to say the most insolent things in the most amiable way. The patron of the arts roared with laughter, his guests tittered; but none of them really enjoyed themselves and they parted in ill-humour. Thus two gentlemen of slight acquaintance meeting on the Nevski Prospect will suddenly grin at one another, affectedly screw up their faces and having passed by will abruptly assume their former indifferent, or gloomy, and for the most part dyspeptic, expressions.

X

ELENA had already left the garden and met Bersyenev in the drawing-room; her welcome was cordial and she at once, almost with impatience, resumed their conversation of the previous day. She was alone; Nikolai Artyomevich had quietly slipped away somewhere and Anna Vassilyevna was lying upstairs with a wet bandage on her head. Beside her sat Zoya, her skirt carefully smoothed and her hands folded on her lap. Uvar Ivanovich was resting in the room under the roof, on a wide, comfortable couch which the family used to call the 'sleep maker'. Bersyenev once more spoke of his father, who to him was a sort of sacred memory. It is time for us also to say a few words about that learned man.

Bersyenev's father had owned an estate of eighty-two serfs, whom he had freed before his death. He was one of the 'Illuminati', a former student of Göttingen, and the author of an unpublished work on 'The Manifestations or Transformations of the Spirit on Earth' – a work in which Schellingianism, Swedenborgianism and Republicanism were blended in a highly original manner. He had come to Moscow while his son was still a child, immediately after the death of his wife, and had himself undertaken the boy's education. He made careful preparations for each lesson, and worked with extraordinary conscientiousness but with a complete lack of success. He was a dreamer, a bookman, a mystic; he had a booming, hesitant way of speaking; he expressed himself obscurely

74

and elaborately, for the most part in analogies, and was actually shy of his own son, whom he loved passionately. It was small wonder that Andrei merely blinked his eyes speechlessly after his lessons and made not the slightest progress. The old man (he was nearly fifty, having married very late) guessed at length that matters were not going as they should, and put him in a boarding-school. Andrei began to learn, though he still did not escape the parental eye; his father visited him continually, wearying the head-master with his talk and instructions; the staff also suffered from the attentions of the uninvited guest who was always bringing them, as they said, profound books on educa-tion. Even the schoolboys felt embarrassed as soon as they saw the old man's dark, pock-marked countenance and the lean figure, invariably garbed in a grey tail-coat of curious cut. The boys did not suspect at the time that the morose and unsmiling old gentleman with the long nose and heron-like gait worried and suffered on account of each one of them, almost as if they had been his own sons. Once he took it into his head to talk to them about Wash-ington. 'Young scholars,' he began – but at the first sound of his strange voice all the young scholars ran away. Life for the honest old student of Göttingen was no bed of roses; he was continually weighed down by the march of history, by questions and problems of every kind.

When young Bersyenev entered the university, his father used to accompany him to lectures; but already his health had begun to fail him. The events of '48 shook him to the foundations of his being (he had to re-write his entire book) and he died in the winter of 1853. He did not live to see his son pass out of the university, but he had already congratulated him on his degree and blessed him in his dedication to the service of science. 'I pass on a torch to you,' he said two hours before his death. 'I carried it as long as I was able; you must not drop it as long as you live.'

For a long time Bersyenev talked to Elena about his father. The sense of embarrassment which he had felt in her presence disappeared, his lisp became less noticeable. The conversation turned to the university.

'Tell me,' Elena asked him, 'among your friends, were there any outstanding people?'

Bersyenev recalled Shubin's words.

'No, Elena Nikolayevna, to tell the truth there wasn't a single outstanding man among us. Far from it. People say that Moscow University had a great day once, but that day certainly isn't now! It's a school now, not a university. I felt rather unhappy about my fellow students,' he added dropping his voice.

'Unhappy?' Elena said softly.

'However,' Bersyenev continued, 'I ought to correct myself. I do know one student – true, he's not doing my course – and he really is an outstanding man.'

'What's his name?' Elena asked eagerly.

'Insarov – Dmítri Nikanorovich Insarov. He's a Bulgarian.'

'Not a Russian?'

'No, not a Russian.'

'Then why does he live in Moscow?'

'He came here to study; and what do you think the real object of his study is? Insarov has only one idea: the liberation of his native land. He's had an extraordinary life, too. His father was a fairly well-to-do merchant, a native of Tirnovo. Today that's only a small town, but in the old days, when Bulgaria was still an independent country, it was the capital. His business was in Sofia, and he had connexions in Russia: his sister, Insarov's aunt, is still living in Kiev, the wife of the senior history teacher in the high school there. Then in 1835, that's eighteen years ago, there was a shocking crime: Insarov's mother suddenly disappeared – and a week later they found her murdered.'

Elena shuddered and Bersyenev stopped.

'Go on, go on,' she said.

'Rumour had it that she had been abducted and murdered by a Turkish official: her husband, Insarov's father, found out the truth and tried to avenge himself – but he only succeeded in wounding the official with a dagger ... They shot him.'

'Shot him? Without a trial?'

'Yes. At the time Insarov was seven years old, and the neighbours took charge of him. His aunt heard about the fate of her brother's family, and asked to have the boy at her home; he was taken to Odessa and from there to Kiev. He spent a full twelve years in Kiev – that's why he speaks Russian so well.'

'So he speaks Russian?'

'As you and I do. When he was twenty – that would be at the beginning of 1848 – he felt he wanted to go back to his own country. He visited Sofia and Tirnovo and roamed the whole length and breadth of Bulgaria; he spent two years there and learnt his native language again. The Turkish government was after him, and he must have been in great peril during those two years. I once noticed he had a long scar on his neck, which was probably the result of a wound: but he doesn't like to talk about these things. Besides, he's a taciturn fellow, in a way. I've tried to draw him out, but it was no use. He just answers in generalities: he's frightfully obstinate. In 1850 he came back to Russia, to Moscow, intending to complete his

77

education, and get to know the Russians thoroughly . . . and then, when he leaves the university . . .'

'What then?' Elena interrupted.

'God knows – it's hard to forecast the future.'

For a long time Elena's eyes remained fixed on Bersyenev's face.

'That's a very interesting story,' she said at last. 'What does he look like, this – what do you call him . . . Insarov?'

'How can I tell you . . . to my way of thinking, not bad-looking. But you'll be able to see for yourself.'

'How do you mean?'

'I shall bring him here to see you. The day after to-morrow he's moving down here to the village; he'll be living with me in the same cottage.'

'Really? But will he want to come and see us?'

'Surely! He'll be very glad to.'

'He's not proud then?'

'He? Not a bit. Or rather, he is proud, but not in the sense you mean. For example, he would never borrow money from anyone.'

'But is he poor?'

'Well, he's not well-off. When he went to Bulgaria he collected such remains of his father's estate as had escaped destruction, and his aunt helps him too: but it all amounts to very little . . .'

'He must be a man with a lot of character,' Elena remarked.

'Yes, he's a man of iron. And at the same time, as you'll see, there's something childlike and frank about him, in spite of all his intense purposefulness and even secretiveness. It's true that his frankness is not our worthless sort, the frankness of people who have nothing whatever to hide – but there, I shall bring him to see you, you must wait.'

'Is he shy?' Elena asked again.

'No, he's not shy. Only thin-skinned people are shy.'

'Are you thin-skinned, then?'

Bersyenev looked embarrassed and made a gesture with his hands.

'You've stirred up my curiosity,' Elena continued. 'But tell me, did he get his revenge on that Turk?'

Bersyenev smiled.

'Only people in novels get their revenge, Elena Nikolayevna; besides, in twelve years the Turk might have died.'

'But Mr Insarov never said anything to you about it?'

'Nothing at all.'

'Why did he go to Sofia?'

'His father lived there.'

Elena mused.

'To liberate his native land,' she said; 'merely to say the words fills one with a feeling of awe – they are such great words.'

At this moment Anna Vassilyevna came into the room and the conversation was cut short.

Bersyenev was strangely agitated as he walked home that evening. He did not regret his decision to introduce Insarov to Elena; it seemed quite natural that his story of the young Bulgarian should have made a deep impression on her – had not he himself tried to strengthen that impression? But something dark and secret had entered his heart; he was sad with an unpleasant sort of sadness . . . However, this melancholy mood did not prevent him from taking up the *History of the Hohenstaufen* at the page where he had left it on the previous evening.

XI

Two days later Insarov, in accordance with his promise, appeared at Bersyenev's cottage with his belongings. He had no servant, but without assistance he proceeded to arrange the furniture, tidy up and dust the room and sweep the floor. A long time was devoted to the desk, which at first refused to fit into the section of the wall appointed for it; but Insarov, with that quiet determination which was peculiar to him, had his way in the end. When he had settled in, he asked Bersyenev to accept ten roubles in advance, and then, arming himself with a stout stick, set off to inspect the surroundings of his new home. He returned after some three hours, and Bersyenev invited him to share a meal with him; he replied that he would not refuse an invitation to dine for that day, but that he had already talked it over with the landlady, and in future would obtain his food from her.

'But you'll be abominably fed,' Bersyenev objected: 'that peasant woman hasn't any idea how to cook. Why don't you want to have your meals with me? We could share the cost.'

'My means don't permit me to eat as you do,' Insarov answered with a quiet smile.

There was something in that smile which did not allow of further insistence on Bersyenev's part; he said no more. After dinner he suggested that they should go to the Stahovs; but Insarov replied that he intended to devote the whole evening to writing letters to his Bulgarian friends and so asked Bersyenev to postpone the visit to another day. Bersyenev was already aware of Insarov's inflexible will, but only now, when he was living under the same roof, did he realize once and for all that Insarov never reversed a decision, just as he never failed to carry out a promise he had made. To Bersyenev, who was essentially Russian, this more than Teutonic meticulousness seemed somewhat odd at first, even a little funny; but he soon accustomed himself to it, and in the end decided that it was at least very convenient, if indeed not creditable.

On the day after his move, Insarov got up at four o'clock in the morning, walked quietly almost all the way round Kuntsovo, bathed in the river, drank a glass of cold milk and then set to work. And in fact he had plenty of work to do: he was studying Russian history and law and political economy, he was translating Bulgarian songs and chronicles, he was collecting material on the Balkan question, he was writing a Russian grammar for Bulgarians and a Bulgarian grammar for Russians. Bersyenev called in to see him and began to discuss Feuerbach. Insarov listened attentively; his comments were infrequent but to the point, and from them it was clear that he was trying to settle in his own mind whether he ought to study Feuerbach or whether he could do without him. Bersyenev led the talk on to Insarov's work and asked whether he would not show him something: Insarov read him his translations of two or three Bulgarian songs and asked his opinion of them. Bersyenev thought that the translations were accurate, but not sufficiently lively, and Insarov noted his comments. From the songs, Bersyenev went on to the contemporary situation in Bulgaria, and it was here that he noticed for the first time the change that came over Insarov at the mere mention of his native country. It was not that his face flushed or that he raised his voice – not that at all: but his whole being seemed to gather strength and urgency, the line of his lips became keener and more ruthless, and a dull unquenchable fire began to glow in the depths of his eyes. Insarov did not care to expatiate on his own journey to his country, but about Bulgaria in general he would gladly talk to anyone. He spoke with unhurried deliberation of the Turks, of their tyranny, of the sorrow and wretchedness of his own people, and of their hopes; his concentrated brooding over a single long-felt passion was evident in every word.

'I'm very much afraid,' Bersyenev thought, as the Bulgarian was speaking, 'I really am afraid that Turk has had to pay dearly for the death of Insarov's father and mother.'

Insarov was still talking when the door opened and Shubin appeared on the threshold.

He came into the room with perhaps a little too much geniality, too much jauntiness; Bersyenev, who knew him well, at once realized that he was on edge.

'I'll introduce myself without ceremony,' he said, with a cheerful, open expression on his face; 'the name is Shubin, I'm a friend of this young man here.' (He indicated Bersyenev.) 'You must be Mr Insarov, aren't you?'

'I am Insarov.'

'Shake hands, then . . . and let's get to know one another. I don't know whether Bersyenev has spoken to you about me, but he's told me a lot about you. So you've come to stay here? Splendid! You mustn't mind me staring at you like this. I'm a sculptor by profession and I can see that I shall soon be asking permission to model your head.'

'My head is at your service,' Insarov said.

'What are we going to do today, eh?' Shubin said, sitting down suddenly on a low chair, his knees wide apart and arms resting on them. 'Andrei Petrovich, has your Lordship any plan for today? We must think of something amusing. The weather's glorious; the smell of the hay and the dried strawberries is like ... it's as if you were drinking strawberry tea. Let's show the new resident of Kuntsovo all the manifold beauties of the place.' ('Something has upset him,' Bersyenev was still thinking.) 'Well, why this silence, Horatio, my friend? Open your prophetic lips: shall we do something or not?'

'I don't know how Insarov feels about it.' Bersyenev said. 'I think he was getting ready to do some work.'

Shubin turned on his chair.

'Are you wanting to work?' he asked, in an affectedly nasal tone.

'No,' the other said; 'I can devote today to walking.'

'Then that's fine,' Shubin said. 'Now come along, Andrei Petrovich, my friend, cover that sage pate of yours with a hat, and we'll wander as far as the eye can see – our eyes are young, and they can see a long way. I know a nasty little inn where they'll give us a beastly little meal, and we'll all enjoy ourselves thoroughly. Come along.'

Half an hour later the three of them were walking along the banks of the Moscow River. Insarov produced a rather odd cap with ear-pieces, which sent Shubin into exaggerated raptures of delight. Insarov walked unhurriedly, looking, breathing, talking and smiling with an air of serenity: this day he had given up entirely to pleasure and he was enjoying it to the utmost. 'Like good little boys going for a walk on Sundays,' Shubin whispered in Bersyenev's ear. Shubin himself played the fool; he ran on in front, imitated the poses of well-known statues, turned somersaults in the grass; Insarov's calm manner, though not exactly irritating him, made him want to clown.

'Whatever are you so restless for, Frenchman?' Bersyenev asked him more than once.

'You're right, I am French, half French,' Shubin retorted, 'so I always have to maintain a balance between jest and earnest, as a certain waiter used to tell me.'

They turned away from the river and proceeded along a narrow sunken path between two tall walls of golden rye, which cast a blue-tinged shadow on them as they walked; the radiant sunshine seemed to be skimming along the tops of the ears of corn; the larks were singing, the quails calling; all around the grass gleamed green, lifted and stirred by a warm breeze, and the flowers were swaying on their stems. For a long time they walked and talked and rested; at one point Shubin actually tried to play leapfrog with a toothless old peasant who was passing by, but whatever they did with him, the old man just giggled; and then they finally came to the 'nasty little inn'. A clumsy servant almost knocked them all over – and did in fact bring them a wretched meal with some kind of South Balkan wine; all this, however, did not prevent them from making merry to their hearts' content, as Shubin had said they would. Shubin himself was the most boisterous in his merriment, and the least genuine: he drank the health of Venelin, a great but obscure personage, and of the Bulgarian King Krum, Hrum or Hrom, who lived, as he said, almost at the same time as Adam.

'In the ninth century,' Insarov corrected him.

'Oh, in the ninth century,' Shubin exclaimed. 'Isn't that wonderful!'

Bersyenev noticed that in the middle of all his joking and fooling, Shubin seemed to be examining Insarov, to be probing him, as if his mind were agitated about something – but Insarov remained placid and serene, as before.

At last they returned home, changed their clothes and, in order not to lose touch with the mood which they had maintained since morning, they decided to go to the Stahovs that evening. Shubin ran on ahead to announce their coming.

XII

'INSAROV the Hero is about to honour us with his presence,' he cried solemnly, going into the Stahovs' drawing-room. At the moment only Elena and Zoya were there.

'Who?' Zoya asked in German; when she was taken unawares she always spoke in her own language. Elena drew herself up stiffly and Shubin looked at her with a playful smile. She felt annoyed, but said nothing.

'You heard me,' he repeated, 'Mr Insarov is coming.'

'I heard you,' she answered, 'and I heard what you called him. You really astonish me. Mr Insarov hasn't set foot in the house yet, but already you find it necessary to attitudinize about him.'

Shubin was suddenly deflated.

'You're right, you're always right, Elena Nikolayevna,' he muttered. 'But I didn't mean anything, honestly. We've been walking with him the whole day, and I assure you, he's an excellent fellow.'

'I didn't ask you about that,' Elena said, getting up.

'Is Mr Insarov young then?' Zoya asked.

'He's a hundred and forty-five,' Shubin answered irritably.

The page-boy announced the arrival of the two friends and they came into the room; Bersyenev introduced Insarov. Elena asked them to be seated and herself sat down while Zoya went upstairs to warn Anna Vassilyevna. The conversation which ensued was trivial enough, like all first conversations. Shubin looked on from a corner in silence, but there was really nothing particular to be seen. In Elena he observed signs of suppressed irritation with him, Shubin – and that was all. He looked at Insarov and Bersyenev and, in the way of a sculptor, compared their faces. Neither, he thought, was good-looking in himself; the Bulgarian's face had character, was sculpturesque and just now it was well lighted; the Russian seemed rather to call for the art of the painter; there were no strong lines there, but there was personality. But when all was said, a girl might well fall in love with either of them. She wasn't in love yet, but she would come to love Bersyenev: that was his conclusion.

Anna Vassilyevna appeared in the drawing-room and the conversation took on a thoroughly 'country villa' character – with the emphasis on 'villa' and not on 'country'. It was a conversation with plenty of variety, judged by the large number of subjects discussed – but it was interrupted by short, wearisome pauses every three minutes. In one of these pauses, Anna Vassilyevna appealed to Zoya; and Shubin, understanding her silent signal, pulled a wry face. Zoya sat down at the piano and ran through all her songs and piano pieces. Uvar Ivanovich was on the point of appearing from behind the door – but he waggled his fingers and withdrew. After that tea was served, and then everyone took a stroll in the garden . . . It began to grow dark and the guests departed.

In fact, Insarov made less impression on Elena than she herself had expected: or, more accurately, he had not made the kind of impression she had expected. She liked his bluntness and lack of constraint, and she liked his looks; but Insarov as a person, with his quiet resoluteness and unvarnished simplicity, somehow did not fit in with the image

87

of him which had formed itself in her mind on the strength of Bersyenev's stories. Elena, without herself suspecting it, was expecting something more 'fatal'. 'But today,' she thought, 'he spoke very little. That was my fault – I didn't ask him any questions: we must wait for another time. But his eyes are expressive, and honest!' She did not feel that she wanted to revere him, but to offer him a friendly hand – and this puzzled her: not thus had she imagined people like Insarov, this was not her vision of a hero . . . That last word reminded her of Shubin, and as she lay there – she was already in bed – she flushed in anger.

'How did you like your new friends?' Bersyenev asked Insarov on the way back.

'I liked them very much,' Insarov answered. 'Particularly the daughter. I should think she's a nice girl. She's emotional – but her emotion is good.'

'You must go and see them often,' Bersyenev remarked.

'Yes,' Insarov answered, and said nothing more until they reached home. There he at once shut himself in his room; but he kept a candle burning till long past midnight.

Bersyenev had not had time to read through a page of Raumer when a handful of gravel rattled against the window-panes. He started involuntarily, opened the window, and saw Shubin standing there pale as a sheet.

'What a tireless fellow you are, you're like a moth in the night!' Bersyenev was just beginning.

'Sh!' Shubin interrupted him. 'I've come here on the quiet, like Max to Agatha. It's essential for me to have a word with you alone.'

'Then come into the room.'

'No, it's not necessary,' Shubin retorted, and leaned his elbows on the window-frame. 'It's more fun like this, more in the Spanish style. In the first place, I congratulate you:

your stock's gone up. Your much-vaunted, exceptional human being has *failed*! I'm able to guarantee that. And to prove my objectivity in the matter, just listen; here's my certificate of character for Mr Insarov. Talent, none; poetry, a blank; capacity for work, any amount; memory, terrific; intelligence, lacks depth and versatility but is sound and lively; dour and energetic, with even a gift of speech when the subject is his – between you and me – extremely boring Bulgaria . . . What? You think I'm being unjust? . . . Another thing: you'll never be on really familiar terms with him, and no one has ever been on really familiar terms with him. As for me, as an artist I'm repugnant to him, and I'm proud of it. Dour, dour, but he's capable of crushing us all to dust. He's tied to his native soil: not like us, poor, weak, empty vessels, trying to ingratiate ourselves with the common people, so that the living water may be poured into us. On the other hand, his problem is easier, more straightforward: all he's got to do is to turn out the Turks, that's all there is to it! But, thank God, none of these qualities are what women like! He's no fascination, no charm, such as you and I have got!'

'Why bring me into it?' Bersyenev muttered. 'And you're wrong about the rest of it: you're not at all repugnant to him, and he's on very intimate terms with his own people . . . I know that.'

'That's another matter: to them he's a hero – though I must confess I've always imagined heroes to be different from him; a hero doesn't need to know how to talk, he just bellows like a bull; but then he's only got to give a shove with his horns, and the walls crash down. And he doesn't himself have to know why he does it, he just does it. However, it may be that nowadays heroes of a different calibre are called for.'

'Why are you so concerned about Insarov?' Bersyenev asked. 'Did you really come running here merely to give me a description of his character?'

'I came here,' Shubin said, 'because I was very depressed at home.'

'So that's it! You're not going to start weeping again?'

'You may laugh! I came here because I feel I could kick myself, because despair and anger and jealousy are gnawing my heart –'

'Jealousy? Whom are you jealous of?'

'Of you, and him, and everybody. I'm tormented by the thought that if I had understood her sooner, that if, knowing how, I'd gone ahead with it . . . but what's the point of talking. It will just end with me going on perpetually laughing and playing the fool and attitudinizing, as she says, and then going and hanging myself . . .'

'Oh no, you won't hang yourself,' Bersyenev remarked.

'Not on a night like this, of course; but just wait till autumn. Anyway, on a night like this people only die of happiness . . . Oh, happiness! Tonight every shadow that the trees cast across the road seems to be whispering: "I know where happiness is – shall I tell you?" I would have asked you to go for a walk – but I can see that you're in a prosaic mood just now. Go to sleep – and may you dream about mathematical symbols! But as for me, my heart's breaking. Oh, you clever gentlemen, you see a fellow laughing, and you think that means he's light-hearted; you prove that he's contradicted himself, and that means he's not suffering . . . God help you!'

Shubin abruptly left the window. 'Annushka!' Bersyenev was on the point of calling after him, but refrained:

Shubin really did look very upset. A minute or two later Bersyenev actually thought he heard sobbing: he got up and opened the window, but all was silent; only far away someone, probably a passing peasant, was singing a song of the steppes.

XIII

DURING the first two weeks after Insarov moved into the neighbourhood of Kuntsovo, he did not visit the Stahovs more than four or five times; Bersyenev went to see them every other day. Elena was always glad to see him, and an interesting, lively conversation always developed between them; nevertheless he often returned home with a downcast expression on his face. Shubin hardly showed himself at all, applying himself to his art with feverish energy; he would shut himself up in his room, popping out occasionally in his blouse, all smeared with clay; or he would stay for days on end in Moscow, where he had a studio, and was visited by the models and Italian mould-makers, who were his friends and teachers. Elena never once talked to Insarov as she would have liked to do; in his absence she would get ready to question him about many things, but when he came she felt ashamed of her preparations. The very calmness of Insarov's manner embarrassed her; she felt she had no right to compel him to speak out, and she decided to wait. In spite of all this, and however trivial were the words which they exchanged, she felt that with each of his visits she was more and more attracted by him; but it never happened that she was left alone with him – and to get to know a person well you must at least have one *tête-à-tête* with him. With Bersyenev she talked about him a great deal. Bersyenev saw that her imagination had been struck by Insarov, and he was glad that his friend had not 'failed', as Shubin maintained. He told her everything he knew about him, enthusiastically and in the utmost detail (we often praise our friends when talking to someone we want to impress, seldom suspecting that by this means we are also praising ourselves); only occasionally, when Elena's cheeks coloured a little, and her eyes widened and brightened, would that unpleasant feeling of melancholy and sadness which he had experienced already begin to oppress him.

One day Bersyenev called on the Stahovs not at his usual time, but soon after ten o'clock in the morning. Elena met him in the lounge.

'What do you think?' he began, with a forced smile. 'Our friend Insarov has disappeared.'

'How do you mean, disappeared?' Elena said.

'Disappeared – he went off somewhere the day before yesterday, and he hasn't been seen since.'

'Didn't he tell you where he was going?'

'No.'

Elena sat down.

'He's probably gone to Moscow,' she said, trying to appear indifferent, and at the same time surprised at herself that she should try to appear indifferent.

'I don't think so,' Bersyenev replied – 'he didn't go alone.'

'Who with, then?'

'The day before yesterday, after dinner, two fellows turned up to see him – probably fellow-countrymen of his.'

'Bulgarians? What makes you think so?'

'Because, so far as I could make out they were talking to him in a language I don't know, but it was certainly Slav ... You always say, Elena Nikolayevna, that there's nothing particularly mysterious about Insarov; but, after all, what could be more mysterious than this visit? Just consider: they went in to his room – and then off they go shouting and arguing, and with such violence and bitterness – Insarov too.'

'He too?'

'Yes, he was shouting at them. They seemed to be blaming one another. And if you'd only seen these visitors! They were both over forty, and had dark, stupid faces with wide cheek-bones and hook-noses, and they were shabbily dressed, dusty and sweaty. They looked like workmen – yet they weren't really workmen or gentlefolk either – God knows what they were.'

'And he went away with them?'

'Yes: he gave them some food and went away with them. The landlady told me that they'd eaten a huge pot of porridge between them; they seemed to be racing to get it down, like wolves.'

Elena smiled faintly.

'You'll see,' she said, 'it will all turn out to be something quite prosaic.'

'I hope to God you're right. But you were wrong to use that word: there's nothing prosaic about Insarov, even though Shubin maintains that there is.'

'Shubin,' Elena broke in, and shrugged her shoulders. 'But you must admit that these two gentlemen, gulping down their porridge . . .'

'Even Themistocles took food on the eve of Salamis,' Bersyenev remarked, smiling.

'Yes: but then there was a battle the next day – but you might let me know when Insarov gets back,' Elena added, and tried to change the subject; but the conversation flagged.

Zoya came into the room and began walking about on

tiptoe, thus indicating that Anna Vassilyevna was still asleep. Bersyenev took his leave.

That same evening Elena received a note from him.

'He's returned,' Bersyenev wrote, 'sunburnt and covered in dust from head to foot. But where he went to and why, I don't know! I wonder if you'll find out.'

'Will I find out!' muttered Elena. 'As if Insarov talks to me!'

XIV

THE next day, shortly after one o'clock, Elena was standing in the garden in front of a box in which she was rearing two mongrel puppies. (The gardener had found them abandoned under the garden fence and had brought them in to her, the washerwoman having told him that the young lady was fond of any sort of animal, wild or tame. He had not erred in his calculation; she gave him a quarter of a rouble . . .) She peeped into the box to make sure the puppies were alive and well, and that fresh straw had been put down for them: then she turned round and almost uttered a cry. Insarov was coming straight towards her along the avenue, alone.

'Good morning,' he said, approaching her and taking off his cap. She noticed that he had in fact got very sunburnt in the last few days. 'I meant to come with Andrei Petrovich, but something delayed him, so I started without him – there's no one about in the house, they're all asleep or out walking, so I came into the garden.'

'You seem to be apologizing,' Elena answered, 'that's quite unnecessary. We're all of us very glad to see you. Let's sit down on the seat, in the shade.'

She sat down, and Insarov took a seat beside her.

'It seems you've not been at home just recently,' she said.

'No,' he replied, 'I went away. Did Andrei Petrovich tell you?'

Insarov looked at her, smiled, and began to play with his cap. As he smiled he blinked rapidly and thrust out his lips, and this somehow gave him an air of great good-humour.

'Probably Andrei Petrovich also told you that I went away with some ... pretty ruffianly people,' he said, still smiling.

Elena was somewhat taken aback, but she felt at once that with Insarov one always had to speak the truth.

'Yes,' she said firmly.

'So what did you think of me, then?' he asked her suddenly.

Elena looked up at him.

'I thought,' she said, 'I thought you always knew what you were doing, and you weren't capable of doing anything bad.'

'Well, thanks for that. You see, Elena Nikolayevna,' he said, moving towards her on the seat, in a confiding sort of way, 'there's a small group of our people here and among us there are some that haven't had much education; but we're all firmly devoted to the common cause. Unfortunately you can't avoid disputes – but they all know me and trust me, and so they sent for me to settle a quarrel. So off I went.'

'Did you go far from here?'

'Sixty versts – to Troitsky. There are some of us there too, attached to the monastery. Anyway, it wasn't trouble for nothing. I settled the business.'

'Was it difficult?'

'Yes. One of them kept being obstinate. Wouldn't repay some money.'

'What? Was the quarrel about money?'

'Yes, and it wasn't much either. But what did you think it was about?'

'And you travelled sixty versts for a trifle like that? You gave up three days?'

'It isn't a trifle, Elena Nikolayevna, when your own people are involved. Then it's a crime to refuse. I see that you yourself don't refuse help even to puppies and I admire you for it. As for the time I lost, that's no matter; I shall make it up later. Our time doesn't belong to us.'

'Who does it belong to then?'

'To all who need us. The reason I've suddenly blurted all this out to you is that I value your opinion of me. I can imagine how Andrei Petrovich must have surprised you.'

'You value my opinion,' Elena said, in a low voice. 'Why?'

Insarov smiled again.

'Because you're a good woman, and not one of these aristocrats . . . that's all.'

There was a short pause.

'Dmitri Nikanorovich,' Elena said, 'do you know this is the first time you've been so frank with me?'

'How do you mean? I think I've always told you whatever was in my mind.'

'No, this is the first time, and I'm very glad it's happened – I want to be frank with you, too. May I?'

Insarov laughed and said: 'You may.'

'I warn you, I'm very inquisitive.'

'Never mind, go on.'

'Andrei Petrovich has told me a lot about your life and childhood. I know one thing that happened, a terrible thing . . . And then later I know that you went back to your own country . . . For heaven's sake don't answer me if it's an indiscreet question – but there's a thought that torments me ... tell me, did you meet that man? ...'

Elena caught her breath. She felt ashamed and aghast at her own audacity. Insarov looked at her steadily, screwing up his eyes a little, and fingering his chin.

'Elena Nikolayevna,' he said at last – his voice was quieter than usual, and that almost frightened her – 'I know who it is you are thinking of. No, I didn't meet him – thank God! I didn't look for him; not because I didn't feel justified in killing him – I would have killed him quite calmly – but because there's no place for private revenge when it's a question of a whole nation avenging itself – no, that's not the right word – when it's a question of a nation liberating itself. The one would be a hindrance to the other. In due course that will come too ... that will come too,' he repeated, nodding his head.

Elena gave him a sidelong glance.

'You love your country very much?' she said timidly.

'I don't know yet,' he replied. 'When a person dies for his country, then you can say he loves it.'

'So that if you lost the chance of going back to Bulgaria,' Elena continued, 'life would be very burdensome for you in Russia?'

Insarov looked down.

'I don't think I could bear it,' he said.

'Tell me,' Elena began again, 'is it difficult to learn Bulgarian?'

'Not at all. A Russian ought to be ashamed not to know Bulgarian. A Russian ought to know all the Slav dialects. Would you like me to bring you some Bulgarian books? You'll see how easy it is. We have such wonderful songs! As good as the Serbian. But just wait, I'll translate one of them for you. It's about . . . You know at least a little of our history?'

'No, I don't know any,' Elena replied.

'Wait, I'll bring you a book. You'll get the main facts from it, at least. Now just listen to this song . . . But perhaps I'd better bring you a written translation. I'm certain you'll love us – you love everyone that's oppressed . . . If you only knew how rich our countryside is! And yet they're trampling on it and tormenting it,' he broke out with an involuntary movement of his arm, and his face darkened. 'They've taken everything from us, everything: our churches, our rights, our land. They've hunted us like cattle and slaughtered us, the Turkish swine.'

'Dmitri Nikanorovich!' Elena cried.

He stopped.

'Forgive me. I can't talk about this coolly. But you were just asking me if I loved my country. What else is there to love in all the world? What is the one unchanging thing, the one thing that transcends every doubt, the one thing you can't help believing in, after God? And when this country has need of you . . . Mark this: the last peasant, the last beggar in Bulgaria and I – we all want the same thing. We all have the same aim. You must realize what confidence and strength this gives us.'

Insarov was silent for a moment and then started talking about Bulgaria again. Elena listened to him with absorbed attention, thoughtful and sad. When he had finished she asked him again:

'So you wouldn't stay in Russia, not for anything?'

When he went away she gazed after him for a long time. He had become another person for her that day; the man to whom she said 'good-bye' was not the same man that she had greeted two hours earlier.

From that day he began to visit them more and more often, while Bersyenev came less frequently. Something strange grew up between the two friends, something they both felt but could not name, and feared to explain. And so a month passed by.

XV

ANNA VASSILYEVNA liked to stay in her own home, as the reader is already aware; but occasionally, quite unexpectedly, she was filled with an irresistible longing for something unusual, for some really striking *partie de plaisir*; and the greater the difficulties associated with this outing, and the greater the amount of preparation and organization it called for, and the greater the degree to which Anna Vassilyevna was herself agitated by it – so much the more agreeable she found it. If this mood happened to take her in the winter she would book two or three boxes in a row, collect all her friends together, and go to a theatre or even a masked ball; in the summer she would go for a trip out of town, the further the better. The next day she would complain of a headache, and groan, and keep to her bed; but in a couple of months the longing for something 'out of the ordinary' would flare up again. And this was just what occurred now: someone happened to mention the beauties of Tsaritsino in her presence, and she promptly announced that she intended to visit Tsaritsino 'the day after tomorrow'. At that there was a great commotion throughout the household: a messenger galloped off to Moscow to fetch Nikolai Artyomevich; the butler galloped with him to buy wine, meat pies and various provisions; Shubin received instructions to hire a chaise (one carriage would not have been enough) and to order the relay horses to be in readiness; twice the page-boy ran round to Bersyenev and Insarov, each time bearing an invitation written out by Zoya, the first in Russian, the second in French; while Anna Vassilyevna busied herself with what the young ladies were going to wear on the journey.

Meanwhile the whole project almost collapsed; Nikolai Artyomevich arrived back from Moscow in a sour, spiteful, 'frondeurish' state of mind (he was still sulking at Avgustina Christianovna) and, as soon as he heard what it was all about, he announced firmly that he wasn't going; he said it was ridiculous to drive from Kuntsovo to Moscow and from Moscow to Tsaritsino and then from Tsaritsino back to Moscow and from Moscow back to Kuntsovo; and finally he added that if they could prove to him that it was any pleasanter on one point of the earth's surface than on another, he would go with them. No one, of course, was able to prove this, and Anna Vassilyevna, not having a suitable escort, was ready to give up the party, when she remembered Uvar Ivanovich. 'A drowning man will clutch at a straw,' she observed, and in desperation sent for him to his room. He was woken up and came downstairs; he listened in silence to Anna Vassilyevna's proposal, waggled his fingers and, to the astonishment of all, agreed. Anna Vassilyevna kissed him on the cheek and called him a dear. Nikolai Artyomevich smiled scornfully and said 'Quelle bourde' (he liked on occasion to make use of 'smart' French expressions) – and the following morning at seven o'clock the carriage and chaise, each fully laden, rolled out of the courtyard of the Stahovs' villa. In the carriage sat the ladies, with Bersyenev and a maid, while Insarov sat on the box; Shubin and Uvar Ivanovich were in the chaise. Uvar Ivanovich, with a movement of one finger, had beckoned Shubin to come with him; he knew that Shubin would be teasing him all the way, but there existed between the 'spirit of the black earth' and the young artist a sort of queer bond, an abusive frankness. However, this time Shubin left his fat friend in peace; he was quiet, mild-mannered and absent-minded.

The sun was already high in a cloudless azure sky when the carriages drove up to the ruined castle of Tsaritsino, which was of sombre and threatening aspect even at midday.

They all got out on to the grass and at once proceeded into the grounds. Elena and Zoya walked in front with Insarov; behind came Anna Vassilyevna on Uvar Ivanovich's arm, with an expression of complete bliss on her face. Uvar Ivanovich panted as he jogged along; his new straw hat cut into his forehead, his feet were burning in his boots, but he felt contented nevertheless. Shubin and Bersyenev brought up the rear. 'We'll be in the reserve, like the veterans, my friend,' Shubin whispered to Bersyenev. 'Now Bulgaria's in the van,' he added, nodding towards Elena.

The weather was marvellous. All around there was blossom and song and the hum of insects; the lakes gleamed in the distance; a gay festive mood took possession of them all. 'Oh, how grand it is, how grand,' Anna Vassilyevna kept repeating; Uvar Ivanovich nodded his head approvingly in response to her exclamations of delight and once actually managed to say: 'Words fail me!' Elena occasionally exchanged a few remarks with Insarov; Zoya held on to the brim of her broad hat with two fingers, and coquettishly poked out her small feet, in their light grey boots, from beneath her pink silk dress, looking now to her side, now over her shoulder. 'Aha!' Shubin exclaimed suddenly in an undertone, 'there's Zoya looking round; I'll go and join her. Elena Nikolayevna disdains me nowadays –

and she esteems you, Andrei Petrovich, which comes to the same thing. I'll go along, I've had enough of this. As for you, my friend, I recommend you to study the wild flowers; that's the best thing you can do in your situation; besides, it's valuable from the scientific point of view. Farewell.' He ran towards Zoya and offered her his arm; '*Ihre Hand*, madam,' he said, and whisked her on ahead. Elena stopped, called Bersyenev, and likewise took his arm; but she continued her conversation with Insarov. She asked him what they called the lily of the valley in his own language, and the oak, the maple and the lime tree ... 'Ah, Bulgaria!' thought the unhappy Andrei.

A sudden cry was heard from in front and everyone looked up. Zoya had seized Shubin's cigar-case and sent it flying into a bush. 'Just you wait, I'll get even with you for that,' he cried, scrambling after it. He found the cigar-case and returned to her side; but no sooner had he reached her than the case went spinning across the path again. Some five times the trick was repeated, Shubin laughing and threatening her all the while, and Zoya merely smiling slyly and shrugging her shoulders like a kitten. Finally he caught hold of her fingers and squeezed them so hard that she squealed aloud; for a long time afterwards she blew on her hands and pretended to be annoyed, while he chanted something into her ear.

'The mischievous youngsters,' Anna Vassilyevna observed gaily to Uvar Ivanovich: he waggled his fingers.

'What do you think of Zoya Nikitishna?' Bersyenev asked Elena.

'What do you think of Shubin?' she answered.

Meanwhile the party approached the Milovidova summer-house and stopped there to admire the view of the Tsaritsino lakes. They were spread out one behind the other over several versts, with the dark, dense woods beyond them. The grass which covered the hillside right down to the principal lake imparted an extraordinarily brilliant emerald colour to the water. There was not a wave, not a sign of foam even by the water's edge; not even a ripple disturbed the smooth unbroken surface. It was as though a heavy, gleaming mass of glass had settled down in some enormous bowl, and the sky had gone to the bottom of it, while the verdurous trees surveyed themselves in its translucent depths. For a long time they admired the view in silence; even Shubin was quiet and Zoya thoughtful. At length, as if all of one mind, they felt they wanted to go for a trip on the water. Shubin, Insarov and Bersyenev raced each other down the grassy slope. They sought out a large painted boat, found a couple of boatmen and summoned the rest of the party. The ladies came down to join them, with Uvar Ivanovich stepping cautiously behind. There was a deal of laughter as he entered the boat and took his seat. 'Mind you don't drown us, sir,' said one of the boatmen, a snub-nosed young fellow in a high-necked shirt. 'Now then, young fellow!' Uvar Ivanovich said. The boat pushed off, and the young men took to the oars; but it turned out that only Insarov knew how to row. Then Shubin proposed that they should sing a Russian song together, and began himself with 'Down Mother Volga'. Bersyenev, Zoya and even Anna Vassilyevna joined in (Insarov was unable to sing) but they were soon out of tune and got mixed up at the third verse; only Bersyenev tried to continue in his bass voice:

'In the waves there was naught to be seen' – but he soon became embarrassed. The boatmen winked at one another and grinned silently. 'It doesn't look as if we knew how to sing, does it?' Shubin said, turning towards them. The lad in the high-necked shirt merely wagged his head. 'Just wait!' Shubin retorted, 'we'll show you! Zoya Nikitishna, sing us *Le Lac* by Niedermeyer – stop rowing, there!' The oars rose in the air like wings and hung motionless while the water dripped melodiously from them; the boat drifted on for a while, then stopped and turned slightly on the water, like a swan. Zoya pretended to be reluctant ... '*Allons,*' said Anna Vassilyevna encouragingly: Zoya threw off her hat and began to sing –

'*O Lac, l'année à peine a fini sa carrière ...*'

Her clear small voice carried across the surface of the water, and every word echoed far away in the woods – it was as though another voice was singing there, clear, mysterious, but not human, not of this earth. As Zoya finished singing there was a loud 'Bravo!' from one of the summer-houses which lay along the side of the lake, and a number of red-faced Germans, who were on the spree at Tsaritsino, came running out – some of them without jacket, tie or waistcoat – and shouted 'Encore' so vociferously that Anna Vassilyevna ordered the boatmen to row to the other end of the lake as quickly as possible. But before the boat reached the bank, it once more fell to Uvar Ivanovich to astonish his friends; observing that one part of the woods produced an exceptionally clear echo, he began to imitate the cry of a quail. At first they were startled, and then genuinely delighted – the more so as Uvar Ivanovich gave a very realistic and accurate rendering. Encouraged by this he attempted to mew like a cat, but here he was not so successful; so he gave one more imitation of the quail, looked at them all, and lapsed into silence. Shubin flung himself on him with a kiss, but Uvar Ivanovich pushed him away. Just then the boat drew up to the bank, and they all got out.

Meanwhile the coachman, the footman and maid had brought the baskets from the carriage, and got lunch ready on the grass under some old lime trees. Everyone sat down round the outspread table-cloth and set to work on the pasties and other viands. They all had excellent appetites, but Anna Vassilyevna kept urging her guests to take a little more, assuring them that it was an excellent thing to eat well in the fresh air, and even appealing to Uvar Ivanovich in like terms. 'Don't worry,' he grunted, with his mouth full. 'What a gloriously fine day God has given us,' she said over and over again; she seemed another person and twenty years younger. Bersyenev told her so. 'Yes, yes,' she said, 'I had my day too, you know. You wouldn't have missed me in a crowd then.' Shubin sat by Zoya and kept pouring wine for her; she would refuse, he would press her to take it, then drink it himself and offer her more; he also protested that he would like to lay his head on her lap, but she was in no way inclined to permit him 'such a liberty'. Elena seemed the most serious of the party, but there was a marvellous peace in her heart, such peace as she had not experienced for many a day; she was suffused with a feeling of infinite goodwill towards everyone, and wanted not only Insarov to sit beside her, but Bersyenev too ... Andrei Petrovich realized vaguely what this meant and sighed secretly.

The hours sped by; evening approached. Anna Vassilyevna suddenly became anxious. 'Oh dear, how late it is,' she said. 'Come, my friends, we've wined and dined, it's time to wipe the crumbs away.' She began fussing about, and everyone began fussing about; then all got up and walked towards the castle where the carriages were waiting. As they passed the lakes they stopped to take another admiring look at Tsaritsino. The rich colours of approaching evening were blazing everywhere, the sky was turning crimson, the leaves, stirred by a rising wind, gleamed in ever-changing hues; the waters of the lakes rippled like molten gold; the red brown of the summer-houses and turrets, dispersed about the grounds, contrasted sharply with the deep green of the trees. 'Good-bye, Tsaritsino, we shall never forget today!' Anna Vassilyevna said . . . But just at that moment, as if to give weight to her last words, something strange took place, something which was in fact not so easy to forget.

What happened was this: hardly had Anna Vassilyevna bid farewell to Tsaritsino than a discordant outburst of shouting and laughter was heard from behind a tall lilac bush a few paces from her – and a whole mob of tousle-headed men, the same mob of musical enthusiasts that had so warmly applauded Zoya, streamed on to the path, apparently in an advanced state of inebriation. They stopped when they saw the ladies; but one of them, a tremendous fellow with a bull-like neck and inflamed animal eyes, stepped out from the rest and, bowing and swaying as he walked, approached the petrified Anna Vassilyevna.

'*Bonjour*, madame,' he said hoarsely, 'how are you?'

Anna Vassilyevna recoiled from him.

'And why didn't you want to sing us an encore,' the giant continued, talking bad Russian, 'when our company kept cheering and shouting "Encore" and "Bravo"?'

'Yes, why didn't you?' his companions echoed.

Insarov was just stepping forward when Shubin stopped him and placed himself protectively in front of Anna Vassilyevna.

'Allow me to express to you, esteemed stranger,' he said, 'the sheer amazement which we all feel at your behaviour. So far as I am able to judge, you belong to the Saxon branch of the Caucasian race, and we must therefore assume that you are aware of the common decencies of life; yet in spite of this you start conversing with a lady to whom you have not been introduced. Be assured that at another time I, as a sculptor, would have particular reason to welcome a closer acquaintance with you, for I observe in you so phenomenal a development of the muscles, of the biceps, the triceps and the deltoid, that I should account it a real pleasure to have you as a model; but for the present, kindly leave us in peace.'

With his head contemptuously cocked on one side and his hands on his hips, the esteemed stranger heard out Shubin's speech.

'I don't understand anything that you have said,' he observed at length. 'Do you think I'm a bootmaker or watch repairer, perhaps? Eh? I'm an officer, I'm an official, yes.'

'I've no doubt of it . . .' Shubin was beginning.

'And I tell you what,' the stranger said, pushing him aside with his powerful arm as if he were a small branch stretched across his path, 'why have you not sung an encore when we have shouted "Encore". And now I shall go away at once this very minute, but first this Fräulein - no, not this madam, not her - but this Fräulein here, or this one' - he pointed to Elena and Zoya - 'must give me *einen Kuss*, as we say it in German, a little kiss, yes; what about it? It is nothing.'

'*Einen Kuss*, it is nothing,' echoed his companions again.

'*Ih! der Sakramenter!*' uttered one thoroughly besotten German, choking with laughter.

Zoya gripped Insarov's arm, but he broke away from her and stood right in front of the huge, insolent fellow.

'Kindly go away,' he said quietly but sharply.

The German laughed heavily.

'Go away? Well, I like this! Can't I make a walk, too? What do you mean, go away? What for?'

'Because you've had the audacity to molest a lady,' Insarov said, and suddenly turned pale. 'Because you're drunk.'

'How? I drunk! Do I hear? *Hören Sie das, Herr Provisor?* I'm an officer, and he has dared to . . . Now then, I demand satisfaction . . . *einen Kuss will ich.*'

'If you take another step forward –' Insarov began.

'Well, and what then?'

'I'll throw you into the water.'

'Into the water? *Herr je!* Is that all? Let's see, then, I'll be interested to know how you . . .'

The 'officer' raised his arms and lurched forward, but at that moment something very strange occurred; he gave a grunt, his huge body tottered suddenly, then rose into the air with his legs kicking; and before the ladies had time to cry out, or anybody could quite make out how it happened, the officer in all his huge bulk plunged with a mighty splash into the lake and disappeared under the swirling water.

'Oh!' shrieked the ladies with one voice.

'*Mein Gott!*' came from the others.

A minute passed . . . then a round head appeared out of the water, with wet hair sticking all over it; bubbles streamed from it and two hands were seen clutching convulsively at its mouth.

'He's drowning, save him, save him!' Anna Vassilyevna shouted to Insarov, who was standing on the bank with his legs apart, breathing heavily.

'He'll swim out,' he remarked, with a contemptuous, unpitying indifference. 'Let's go,' he went on, taking Anna

Vassilyevna's arm. 'Come along, Uvar Ivanovich, and you, Elena Nikolayevna.'

'Ah – oh!' wailed the unfortunate German, who had just succeeded in grasping the reeds growing on the bank.

As they moved off after Insarov they had to pass alongside the mob of Germans; but once deprived of their leader the revellers had quietened down and did not utter a word – except for one, the most audacious of them, who muttered: 'Well . . . my God . . . that's the limit!' . . . while another went so far as to take his hat off. Insarov appeared to them to be a very formidable person – and not without reason: something sinister, something dangerous had come into his expression. The Germans made a rush to pull their comrade out of the water; and as soon as he felt solid earth beneath him the 'officer' began cursing plaintively, shouting after the 'Russian scoundrels' that he would complain about them, that he would see His Excellency Count von Kieseritz himself . . .

But the Russian scoundrels paid no attention to his cries and hurried on to the castle as quickly as possible. They were silent as they passed through the grounds; only Anna Vassilyevna sighed quietly. But as soon as they reached the carriages they stopped and gave way to a prolonged outburst of irrepressible Homeric laughter. A shrill, frantic outburst from Shubin began it, then came Bersyenev's raucous cackle and Zoya's rippling laughter; Anna Vassilyevna began to shake with mirth, even Elena could not help smiling, and in the end Insarov himself gave way also. But the maddest, loudest, longest laughter came from Uvar Ivanovich; he laughed till his sides ached, till he coughed and sneezed. 'I thought to myself,' he said through his tears, growing a little calmer, 'I thought – what's that noise? – and – it's him – flat on his back.' And as he convulsively ejaculated those last words, a new spasm of laughter shook his frame. Zoya added fuel to the fire. 'I could see his legs up in the air,' she said . . . 'Yes, his legs, his legs,' Uvar Ivanovich broke in, 'and then splash . . . flat on his back!' – 'But how did he manage it,' Zoya asked, 'the German was three times his size?' – 'I'll tell you, I saw it,' Uvar Ivanovich said, wiping his eyes; 'he got him by the small of the back with one arm and tripped him up and then . . . what a splash! I heard it: what's that, I thought – and – it's him – flat on his back!'

Long after the carriages had started, and the castle was already out of sight, Uvar Ivanovich was still unable to calm down. At last Shubin, who was again travelling with him in the chaise, managed to make him ashamed of himself.

But Insarov was feeling conscience-stricken. He sat in the carriage opposite Elena (Bersyenev was on the box) and said nothing; she, too, was silent. He thought she was blaming him for what had happened, but she was not. True, she had been very frightened during the first minute or two; then she had been struck by the expression on his face; and then she had begun to think – though she was not quite clear *what* she thought. The emotion which she had experienced during the day had gone – that she realized; but it had given place to something else, something which she still did not understand.

The outing had gone on too long – imperceptibly, evening changed into night. The carriage sped on, now beside fields of ripening corn, where the air was heavy and fragrant with the scent of grain, now beside open meadows whose unexpected freshness surged in gentle waves upon their faces: the sky melted into haze on the horizon; at last a dull red moon came up. Anna Vassilyevna dozed off;

Zoya leaned out of the window and looked at the road. At length it occurred to Elena that she had not spoken to Insarov for more than an hour; she asked him some trivial question; he answered at once, eagerly. Vague sounds began to float on the night air like the murmur of innumerable voices in the distance: Moscow was hurrying to meet them. Ahead of them lights began to glimmer, and grow more numerous; at last the wheels were rattling over cobble-stones. Anna Vassilyevna woke up, and everyone began to talk, though the clatter of the two carriages and thirty-two hooves on the road made it impossible to hear what was said. From Moscow to Kuntsovo the journey seemed long and tedious. They all fell asleep or relapsed into silence, resting their heads in odd corners; Elena alone did not close her eyes, but gazed fixedly at Insarov's form in the darkness. Shubin fell into a state of gloom; a light breeze blew into his eyes and irritated him; he drew the collar of his coat round his neck and for a moment almost wept. Uvar Ivanovich snored happily, swaying from one side to the other. At last the carriages stopped, and two footmen lifted Anna Vassilyevna out; she was quite overcome, and as she bade good night to her companions, asserted that she hardly felt alive; they began to thank her, but she only repeated 'hardly alive'. Elena shook hands with Insarov – it was the first time she had done so; she went to her room and for a long time sat by the window without undressing. As Bersyenev was leaving, Shubin seized an opportunity to whisper:

'You see what I told you, he *is* a hero: he throws drunken Germans into the water.'

'You didn't even do that,' Bersyenev retorted and set off home with Insarov.

Dawn was already showing in the sky when the two

friends reached the cottage. The sun had not yet risen, but the chill of dawn was in the air; a grey dew covered the grass, the first larks were singing high in the twilit vault above them, and like a lonely eye the last bright star looked down.

XVI

SOON after Elena met Insarov she began to keep a diary (it was the fifth or sixth diary she had attempted). Here are some extracts from it:

June . . . Andrei Petrovich keeps bringing me books, but I can't read them. I feel ashamed to confess it to him; yet I don't want to give them back and lie and say I've read them. I think he'll be upset; he always takes such an interest in me. I believe he is much attached to me. He's a very nice man, Andrei Petrovich.

. . . What is it that I really want? Why am I so depressed, so sick at heart? Why do I look so enviously at the birds flying past? I long to fly away with them – where to, I don't know, but somewhere far, far away from here. But isn't this a sinful feeling? I have mother, father, family here – can it be that I don't love them? No, I don't love them as I should wish to; it's terrible to confess it, but it's the truth. Perhaps I'm a great sinner – perhaps that's why I feel so dejected, why I have no peace. Some hidden power holds me and oppresses me. It's as though I'm in a prison, with the walls about to fall down on me. But why don't other people feel like this? Whom shall I ever love, if I feel cold towards my own family? Evidently Papa is right when he reproaches me and says I only love the dogs and cats. I must think about that. I must pray; I pray too little . . . Yet I believe I'm capable of love.

. . . I still always feel shy with Mr Insarov. I don't know why; I'm not a child, and he's so simple and kind. Some-

116

times he looks very serious; he probably has more important things to think about than people like us. I sense this and somehow I feel ashamed of taking up his time. With Andrei Petrovich it's another matter. I'm ready to talk to him for the whole day if need be. But then he always talks to me about Insarov. And what terrifying details! Last night I dreamt I saw him with a dagger in his hand; he was saying: 'I shall kill you and then I shall kill myself.' What foolishness!

Oh, if only someone would tell me: 'This is what you must do.' To be good is not enough; to do good ... yes, that is the real purpose of life. But how is one to do good? Oh, if only I could control myself! I can't understand why I think about Mr Insarov so often. When he comes and sits with us, and listens attentively, so calmly and without making any fuss, I look at him, and it seems pleasant to do so – that's all; but when he goes away I keep thinking of what he said, and I feel angry with myself, and even get quite agitated – I don't know why myself. (He speaks French badly and isn't ashamed of it: I like that about him.) But then I always think a lot about new acquaintances ... While I was talking to him, I suddenly thought of our butler, Vassili, who dragged an old cripple out of a burning hut and almost lost his own life. Papa called him a brave fellow, and Mama gave him five roubles, but I wanted to go down on my knees to him. And he had such a simple, even a stupid, face, and afterwards he took to drink.

... Today I gave a trifle to a beggar-woman and she asked me why I was so sad. And I'd never suspected that my expression was sad. I think it's due to the fact that I'm always alone, alone with my own goodness and wickedness. There's no one to whom I want to stretch out my hand in friendship. Those that come to me I don't need, those that I want pass by.

... I don't know what has come over me today ... My mind is confused, I feel ready to fall on my knees and beg and pray for mercy. I feel as though I'm being murdered, how or by whom I don't know, and inwardly I'm screaming and rebellious; I weep, and I can't be silent. God, God, subdue in me these fits of passion ... only You can do it, all else is powerless. My futile charities, my occupations ... nothing, nothing, nothing can help me. Truly, I should go away and work as a servant girl somewhere: it would be easier for me that way.

... What is youth for, what am I alive for, why do I have a soul, why do I suffer all this?

... I keep thinking of Insarov ... Mr Insarov – I really don't know how I should write it. I wish I knew what was in his heart. He seems to be so open and approachable, and yet nothing is *visible* to me there. Sometimes he looks at me with a sort of searching look – or is that my imagination? Pavel keeps teasing me, and I'm cross with him. What does he expect? He's in love with me – and I don't want his love. He's in love with Zoya too. I'm unjust to Pavel – he told me yesterday that I couldn't be unjust by halves ... That's true. It's very wrong of me.

... Oh, it seems to me that a man needs to be unhappy or poor or sick – otherwise he'll become arrogant.

... Why did Andrei Petrovich tell me about those two Bulgarians today? He seemed to have some reason for it. What's Mr Insarov to me? I feel cross with Andrei Petrovich.

... I take up my pen ... but I don't know how to begin. It was such a surprise when he started talking to me in the garden today! And how kind and confiding he was! And how quickly it all happened! As though we were old, old friends, and had just happened to recognize each other. How was it possible not to understand him before? And how close he is to me now! And this is what is so surprising: I feel much calmer now. It's laughable: yesterday I was angry with Andrei Petrovich, and with Insarov, too – I even called him *Mister* – whereas today ... Well, here's a sincere man at last, a man you can rely on. This one tells the truth; he's the first man I've ever met who doesn't lie: all the others lie, everything lies. Andrei Petrovich, how can I insult you by saying that, dear, kind Andrei? – But no! You may be more learned than he is, cleverer even – but somehow you seem small beside him. When he talks of his country he seems to grow in stature and his face seems finer, his voice takes on a ring of steel and then I don't believe there's a man in all the word he wouldn't look straight in the eyes. And he doesn't only talk – he's done things and is going to do things. I must ask him ... How suddenly he turned and smiled at me! Only brothers smile like that. Oh, how contented I feel. When he came to us first I never thought we should soon be so close to one another. And now I even feel glad that I was indifferent about him when he came the first time ... Indifferent! Can it really be that I'm not indifferent now?

... For a long time I've not felt such inward peace. It's so quiet in my heart, so quiet. There's nothing to write about. I often see him – and that's all. What more is there to say?

... Pavel has shut himself up in his room; Andrei Petrovich has begun to come less often. Poor man; I think he ... however, it couldn't be. I like talking to Andrei Petrovich: there's never a word about himself, but he always talks about something sensible and worth-while. It's not the same with Shubin; he's showy, like a butterfly, and he's proud of showiness – unlike a butterfly. But then, both Shubin and Andrei Petrovich are . . . oh, well, I know what I mean.

. . . *He* likes coming to us, I can tell that. But why? What does he see in me? True, we both have tastes in common: and neither of us cares for poetry or understands art. But how much better he is than me! He is calm, whereas I'm eternally in a tumult; he sees his way clear and has a goal – but where am I going, where shall I find a resting place? Yes, he's calm – but his thoughts are far from here. There'll come a time when he'll leave us all for ever and go away to his own people, over there beyond the sea. Well, God grant him success. Yet in spite of everything I shall be glad I came to know him while he was here.

. . . Why isn't he Russian? No – he couldn't be Russian.

. . . Even Mama likes him – she says he's a modest young man. Dear kind Mama, she doesn't understand him. Pavel keeps quiet; he can guess that I don't like his insinuations about Insarov, but then he's jealous. Spiteful boy! What right has he to be jealous? Have I ever . . .? What nonsense all this is. Why does it come into my head?

. . . But isn't it strange that I'm twenty years old already and have never loved anyone yet? I believe the reason that D. (I'm going to call him D., I like the name Dmitri) is always so calm is because he gives himself up entirely to his work and his ideals. What has he got to worry about? Whoever gives himself up utterly to something . . . utterly – he doesn't need to worry, for he no longer has to answer for anything. Then it's not what *he* wants, but what the cause demands . . . Incidentally, I find we both like the same flowers. I picked a rose today, and one of the petals fell off. He picked it up, and I gave the rose to him.

. . . D. often visits us. Yesterday he stayed the whole evening. He wants to teach me Bulgarian. I feel at ease, at home, with him . . . no, more than at home.

. . . How the days fly . . . I'm happy and somehow a little frightened. First I feel I want to thank God – then to weep. Oh, these warm bright days!

. . . I still feel light at heart, and only occasionally, just occasionally, a little sad. I'm happy – or am I happy?

. . . It will be a long time before I forget yesterday's outing. Such strange, new frightening experiences! When he picked up that gigantic fellow and threw him into the water like a stone – no, *that* didn't frighten me, but *he* frightened me. And afterwards – how sinister his expression was, almost cruel. And the way he said: 'He'll swim out' – that shattered me; evidently I haven't understood him. And then when everyone was laughing, and I was laughing too, how sorry I felt for him. He felt ashamed, I could feel it, he felt ashamed in front of me. He told me so afterwards, in the carriage, when it was dark and I was trying to make him out and feeling afraid of him. Yes, there's no fooling with him, and he knows how to stand up for you, too. But why so much bitterness, why the quivering lips, the fury in his eyes? But perhaps it couldn't be otherwise; perhaps you can't be a man and a fighter and still be mild and gentle. Life's a rough business, he said to me the other day. I repeated that to Andrei Petrovich, but he didn't agree with D. Which of them is right? . . . And then how wonderfully the day began! How nice it was to walk by his side, even though we didn't talk . . . But I'm glad that all that happened. It seems that it had to be.

. . . I feel restless again . . . not quite well.

. . . All these days I've written nothing in this book because I've had no desire to write. I felt that nothing I could write would express what was in my heart ... And what is in my heart? I've had a long conversation with him, which explained a lot to me. He told me his plans (and incidentally I now know why he has that scar on his neck – My God! When I think that he's been condemned to death already, and only just managed to escape, and he's been wounded, too). He feels there's going to be a war, and he's glad of it. And at the same time, I never saw him so sad before. What can he – he! – have to be sad about? Papa returned from town and found us alone together; he gave us rather a strange look. Andrei Petrovich called in; I noticed he was looking very thin and pale. He reproached me, saying that I was treating Shubin too coldly and casually. And I'd completely forgotten about Pavel. When I see him I'll try to make amends. I've no time for him now – or for anyone at all. Andrei spoke to me in a sort of pitying way. What does it all mean? Why is everything so dark and obscure all round me and within me too? I feel as though something mysterious was going on inside me and around me, something – I must find the right word ...

... I didn't sleep last night – and now my head aches. What's the use of writing? He left so soon today and I wanted to talk to him. He seems to be avoiding me. Yes, he is avoiding me!

... I've found the word, it came to me like a flash of light. God have mercy on me! I love him!

XVII

ON the same day that Elena had written those last fateful words in her diary, Insarov was sitting in Bersyenev's room. Bersyenev stood in front of him with a perplexed expression on his face, for Insarov had just informed him that he intended to return to Moscow the very next day.

'But, really,' Bersyenev exclaimed, 'we're just coming to the most beautiful time of year. What will you do in Moscow? It's such an unexpected decision! Or have you had some news?'

'I've not had any news,' Insarov replied, 'but I've thought it over and I can't stay any longer.'

'But how is it possible –'

'Andrei Petrovich,' Insarov said, 'please do me a favour and don't press me. I myself feel very sorry to part company with you, but there's nothing to be done.'

Bersyenev looked at him intently.

'I know you can't be prevailed on to change your mind,' he said at length. 'So it's definite?'

'Absolutely definite,' Insarov replied; then he got up and left the room.

Bersyenev paced about the room, picked up his hat and set off for the Stahovs.

'You've got something to tell me,' Elena said to him, as soon as they were alone.

'Yes; how did you guess?'

'Never mind. Tell me what it is.'

Bersyenev told her of Insarov's decision. Elena turned pale.

'What does it mean?' she managed to say.

'You know,' Bersyenev said, 'that Dmitri Nikanorovich never likes giving an account of his actions. But I think – let us sit down, Elena Nikolayevna, you don't look well – but I think I can guess the real reason for this sudden departure.'

'What is it, what is it?' Elena asked, unconsciously gripping Bersyenev's arm with her cold hand.

'You see, it's like this –' Bersyenev began, with a sad smile. 'How can I explain it to you? I must go back to last Spring, to the time when I was getting to know Insarov better. I met him at the house of a relative of mine; there was a daughter there, a very pretty girl. It seemed to me that Insarov was rather interested in her and I told him so. He burst out laughing and replied that I was mistaken; his heart was unaffected, he said, but if anything like that did happen to him he'd soon be off. He did not want – these were his actual words – the satisfaction of his personal feelings at the expense of his work and duty. "I'm a Bulgarian," he said, "I don't need the love of a Russian."'

'Well, then ... what do you think now?' Elena whispered, involuntarily turning away her head as though she were expecting a blow, but still not letting go her grip on Bersyenev's arm.

'I think,' he said, and he too lowered his voice, 'I think that what I wrongly imagined had happened then, has happened now.'

'That means ... you think – oh, don't torture me,' Elena burst out suddenly.

'I think,' Bersyenev retorted quickly, 'that Insarov has

now fallen in love with a certain Russian girl, and in accordance with his promise is running away.'

Elena gripped his arm still more tightly, and bowed her head lower, as if she sought to conceal from strange eyes the blush of shame which leapt like a flame over her face and neck.

'Andrei Petrovich, you're as kind as an angel,' she said; 'but, tell me, he'll come to say good-bye, won't he?'

'Yes, I'm sure he'll come, because he won't want to go away without . . .'

'Then tell him, tell him . . .'

But the unhappy girl could no longer contain herself; tears streamed from her eyes and she fled from the room.

'So that's how much she loves him,' Bersyenev thought, as he walked slowly home. 'I hadn't expected that; I hadn't expected that it meant so much already. She called me kind' – his thoughts ran on – 'but who can say what feelings, what motives prompted me to tell her all this? But it wasn't out of kindness, not kindness. It was all just this accursed longing to find out whether what I feared was true, whether the dagger was really in the wound. I ought to be satisfied – they've fallen in love, and I helped them . . . "A future intermediary between science and the Russian public," Shubin called me; it seems I was born to be an intermediary. But supposing I'm wrong? No, I can't be wrong . . .'

His heart was bitter, and he could not concentrate on Raumer that evening.

The following day, at about two o'clock, Insarov appeared at the Stahovs. As if by design, there was a visitor in Anna Vassilyevna's drawing-room at the time; she was the wife of a neighbouring priest, and a very good and estimable woman, though she had had a little trouble with the police (she had taken it into her head, in the heat of the day, to bathe in a pond near a road along which the family of some important general used to drive). Elena, whose face had turned deathly pale when she heard Insarov's step, was at first actually rather glad of the presence of a stranger; but then her heart sank at the thought that he might go without having spoken to her alone. For his part, he seemed to be embarrassed, to be avoiding her eyes: 'Can it be that he's going to say good-bye now,' she thought. He was, in fact, just about to address himself to Anna Vassilyevna; but Elena got up hastily and called him aside to the window. Anna Vassilyevna's guest was rather astonished at this behaviour and tried to look round at them; but she was so tightly laced that her corset squeaked every time she moved, and she decided to sit still.

'Listen,' Elena said quickly, 'I know why you've come: Andrei Petrovich has told me what you intend to do. But don't say good-bye to us today, I implore you: come tomorrow, as early as you can, about eleven o'clock: I must talk to you for a minute.'

Insarov bowed his head and said nothing.

'I won't keep you now . . . will you promise to come?'

Again Insarov bowed his head in silence.

'Elena, come here,' Anna Vassilyevna said, 'look at the beautiful hand-bag our visitor has brought.'

'I embroidered it myself,' the priest's wife remarked.

Elena went away from the window.

Insarov was not with the Stahovs for more than a quarter of an hour: Elena watched him surreptitiously. He kept fidgeting, and as before did not seem to know where to look – then he went away in rather an odd manner: he seemed suddenly just to disappear.

126

For Elena the day passed slowly; the long, long night dragged slower still. She would sit on the bed, clasping her knees with her hands and resting her head on them; she would go to the window and press her hot brow against the cold glass thinking, thinking, thinking always the same thoughts, to the point of utter weariness. Her heart seemed to have turned to stone in her breast – or to have vanished altogether, for she was not conscious of it – but her head throbbed violently, her very hair seemed to be on fire and her lips were parched. 'Yes, he will come . . . he never said good-bye to Mama . . . he wouldn't deceive me . . . Can it be true what Andrei Petrovich said? It's not possible. But he never actually promised to come. Can it be true that he's gone from me for ever? . . .' Such were the thoughts which never left her – literally never left her; for they did not come and go and come again but they swept over her continuously like a mist. 'He loves me!' – the thought flashed through her, through all of her; she gazed intently into the darkness and none was there to see the secret smile which played upon her lips – but suddenly she tossed her head and folded her hands behind her neck and once more those other thoughts came over her like a mist. Before morning came she undressed and lay down on her bed, but she could not sleep. The first red rays of the sun broke into the room . . . 'Oh, if he loves me,' she cried out suddenly and, unabashed by the daylight shining on her, opened wide her arms . . .

She rose, dressed, and went downstairs. No one was awake yet in the house. She went into the garden; but there it was so fresh and green and peaceful, the birds twittered so trustfully, the flowers looked up so joyously, that she was struck with a sense of mystery and awe. 'Oh,' she thought, 'if it is true, there's not a blade of grass that's happier than me! But is it true?' She returned to her room and, to pass the time somehow, began to change her dress. But her things slipped from her hand and fell to the ground and she was still sitting half-dressed before her mirror when they called her to breakfast. She went downstairs: her mother noticed how pale she was, but merely observed: 'How nice you look today.' She scanned her up and down and added: 'That dress suits you very well; you should always wear that one if you particularly want to make an impression on someone.' Elena did not reply, and sat down in a corner. Nine o'clock struck: there were still two hours till eleven. Elena took up a book, then her sewing, then the book again; then she determined to walk down one of the avenues a hundred times, and proceeded to do so. For a long time she watched Anna Vassilyevna playing patience – and then looked at the clock: it was still not ten o'clock. Shubin came into the drawing-room; she tried to talk to him, but only apologized, without knowing why . . . It was not that what she said cost her an effort, but every word somehow bewildered her. Shubin leaned towards her – she expected a gibe and looked up: but it was a sad, friendly face that she saw before her. She smiled at that face; Shubin smiled too, and, saying nothing, went out quietly. She wanted to stop him, but for the moment could not think how. At last eleven o'clock struck. She began to wait and wait and listen. She could no longer do anything; she had even ceased to think. Her heart came to life in her and began to beat louder and louder and, oddly enough, the time began to pass more rapidly. A quarter of an hour, half an hour, a few minutes more than half an hour went by, as she thought: then she gave a start to hear the clock strike not twelve but one o'clock. 'He's not coming, he's going away without saying good-bye . . .' the thought seemed to rush to her head and the blood rushed with it. Her breath seemed to stifle her and she wanted to sob . . . She ran to her room and fell down on the bed with her face in her hands.

For half an hour she lay motionless. Tears ran through her fingers on to the pillow. Suddenly she sat up on the bed. Something strange had taken place within her! Her face changed, her tears dried of their own accord, her eyes began to shine. She knit her brows, pressed her lips together. Another half an hour went by. For the last time she listened; was that the sound of the voice she knew? . . . She got up, put on her hat and gloves and threw a cape over her shoulders; then, slipping out of the house unnoticed, she set off with rapid strides along the road leading to Bersyenev's cottage.

XVIII

ELENA walked with her head bowed, her gaze fixed straight ahead of her. She had no fears, she did not consider the wisdom of what she was doing: she wanted to see Insarov once again. She walked on without noticing that the sun had long since gone behind a bank of black, heavy clouds, that the wind was howling fitfully in the trees and blowing her dress about, that the dust rose suddenly into the air and swept like a solid pillar along the road . . . Even when big drops of rain began to fall she did not notice them; but then they came thicker and faster, with flashes of lightning and bursts of thunder. Elena stopped and looked around . . . Luckily, not far from where the storm had caught her, there was an old, tumble-down shrine, built over a ruined well. She ran towards it and took shelter under the low roof. It was pouring in torrents; the sky was completely hidden by clouds. In dumb despair she gazed at the dense screen of falling raindrops. Her last hope of seeing Insarov vanished. An old beggar-woman came into the shrine, shook herself and bowed; then, groaning and grunting, she sat down on the ledge beside the well. Elena put her hand into her pocket; the old woman noticed what she was doing and her face – which had once been beautiful, though now it was yellow and wrinkled – lightened up. 'Thank you, kind lady,' she began. Elena's purse was not in her pocket, but the old woman was already stretching out her hand.

'I've no money with me,' Elena said, 'but take this, it may be of some use to you.'

She gave her her handkerchief.

'And what can I do with your handkerchief, pretty lady?' the woman said. 'Well, perhaps I'll give it to my grand-daughter when she gets married – God bless you for your kindness!'

There was a clap of thunder.

'Jesus Christ have mercy on us,' she muttered, and crossed herself three times. 'But I think I've seen you before,' she added after a pause – 'wasn't it you who gave me alms in church?'

Elena looked closely at her and recognized her.

'Yes, I did,' she replied, 'and then you asked why I was so sad.'

'So I did, dearie, so I did. I was sure I knew you. And you still look so sad, even now. Your handkerchief's wet, too: that must be your tears, I know. Oh, you young people, it's always the same sorrow with you, such a great sorrow!'

'And what is that sorrow, mother?'

'What sorrow? Oh, my good young lady, you can't take me in, an old woman like me. I know why you're grieving, and you're not the only one. I was young once, too, dearie, I went through all those troubles too. Yes. And I'll tell you something for your kindness. If you find a good man and a steady one, stick to him alone; stick to him stronger than death. Yes, if it's to be that way, so be it; if not, then surely God wills it so. Yes ... Why are you looking so surprised? I'm a fortune-teller, you see. Would you like me to take your grief away in your handkerchief? I'll take it away and then it will all be gone. Look, the rain's not falling so fast now. You must wait a little longer, but

I'll be off. It won't be the first time I've got wet. Now don't forget, dearie; sorrows come and sorrows go and they don't leave a trace behind them. God be with you!'

The old woman got up from the ledge, went out of the shrine and went jogging on her way. Elena looked after her in astonishment. 'What does it mean?' she whispered involuntarily.

The rain gradually began to stop, and the sun came out for a moment. Elena was preparing to leave the shelter . . . Suddenly, a few yards from the shrine, she caught sight of Insarov. He was muffled up in his cloak and was walking along the same path as she had come by: he seemed to be hurrying home.

She put her hand on the worn railing of the steps to support herself and tried to call him, but her voice failed her . . . Insarov had already passed by, without raising his head.

'Dmitri Nikanorovich!' she managed to say at last. Insarov stopped suddenly and looked round. At first he did not recognize her, but he approached at once.

'You! You here!' he cried.

She retreated silently into the shrine. He followed her.

'You here?' he repeated.

Still she said nothing, but merely gazed at him intently and somehow tenderly. He looked down.

'Did you come from our house?' she asked.

'No – not from there.'

'No ?' Elena repeated, and tried to smile. 'So this is how you keep your promises? I waited for you all the morning.'

'Remember, Elena Nikolayevna, I made no promise yesterday.'

Elena tried to smile and passed her hand across her face; both her face and her hand were very pale.

'So you wanted to leave us without saying good-bye?'

'Yes,' said Insarov grimly, and his voice was hoarse.

'What? After our talks together, after our friendship, after everything ... so if I hadn't chanced to meet you here' – her voice rose and she paused for a moment – 'you would have gone away like that and never shaken me by the hand for the last time – and it would have been nothing to you?'

Insarov turned away.

'Elena Nikolayevna, please don't talk like that! I'm far from happy as it is. Please believe me – it cost me a great effort to make my decision. If only you knew why –'

'I don't want to know why you're going,' Elena interrupted, fearfully. 'Apparently it has to be so. Apparently we must part. You wouldn't want to hurt your friends for nothing. But do friends really part this way? It's true that we are friends, isn't it?'

'No,' Insarov said.

'What did you say?' Elena asked. A faint flush came to her cheeks.

'It's just because we aren't friends that I'm going away. Don't force me to say what I don't want to, what I'm not going to ...'

'You used to be frank with me,' Elena reproached him gently. 'Do you remember?'

'I was able to be frank then – I had nothing to hide then; but now ...'

'But now?' Elena asked.

'But now ... But now I must go. Good-bye.'

If Insarov had happened to look up at Elena just then he would have noticed that her face was growing brighter in proportion as his own grew darker and more morose; but he gazed obstinately at the ground.

'Well, good-bye, Dmitri Nikanorovich,' she said; 'but since we *have* met, at least give me your hand.'

Insarov stretched out his hand.

'No, I can't even do that,' he said, and turned away once more.

'You can't?'

'No . . . Good-bye.'

He made his way to the door.

'Wait a moment,' Elena said. 'You seem afraid of me . . . But I've more courage than you,' she added, and a sudden slight tremor passed through her body. 'I can tell you why you found me here. Shall I tell you? Do you know where I was going?'

He looked at her in astonishment.

'I was going to see you.'

'Me?'

Elena covered her face.

'You want to force me to say that I love you,' she whispered. 'There – I've said it.'

'Elena,' he cried.

She dropped her hands from her face, glanced at him and fell on to his breast.

He held her close to him, without speaking. He did not need to tell her that he loved her. That single cry, that instant transformation of his whole being, that rise and fall of the breast upon which she reposed so trustfully, that touch of the finger-tips upon her hair – all told her that he loved her. He was silent, and she asked no word of him. 'He is here, he loves me . . . what else is there?' The calm of utter blessedness, the calm of the quiet harbour, of the goal achieved, that divine calm in which death itself finds meaning and beauty, surged over her like a heavenly wave. She asked for nothing because she had everything. 'My brother, my friend, my beloved,' she whispered, and she herself did not know whose heart it was, his or her own, that throbbed and melted away so sweetly in her breast.

He stood motionless, holding in his strong arms this young life which had given itself to him, and he was aware of a new and infinitely sweet burden on his breast – a feeling of tenderness and inexpressible gratitude broke down his unyielding heart, and tears that he had never known before came into his eyes.

But Elena did not cry; she only repeated again and again: 'My brother, my friend!'

'You'll come with me everywhere?' he asked, after a quarter of an hour had passed, still holding her and supporting her in his arms.

'Everywhere – to the end of the world. Wherever you are, I will be there too.'

'And you're not deluding yourself – you know that your parents will never agree to our marrying?'

'I don't delude myself: I know it.'

'You know that I'm poor, almost penniless?'

'Yes.'

'You know that I'm not a Russian, that my destiny is outside Russia, and you'll have to break all your ties with your own country and your own people?'

'I know, I know.'

'And you know too that I've dedicated myself to a hard and thankless task, and that I – that we shall be subjected not only to danger, but possibly privation and humiliation as well?'

'Yes, I know it all . . . I love you.'

'And you'll have to give up all you're accustomed to, and maybe you'll have to work there, alone among strangers?'

She put her hand over his mouth.

'I love you, my darling.'

He kissed her slender, flushed hand ardently; she did not withdraw it from him, but watched with a sort of child-like, amused curiosity how he covered it with kisses.

Suddenly she blushed and hid her face in his bosom.

He lifted her head tenderly and gazed intently into her eyes.

'My wife,' he said, 'my wife before man and God.'

XIX

AN hour later Elena, with her hat in one hand and her cape in the other, quietly entered the drawing-room of the villa. Her hair was a little untidy, there was a touch of colour in her cheeks, the smile still persisted on her lips and her half-closed eyes were smiling also. She could hardly move for weariness, but her very weariness was agreeable to her; indeed, everything was agreeable to her now, everything and everybody seemed to be so kind and affectionate. Uvar Ivanovich was sitting by the window; she went up to him, put her hand on his shoulder and yawned and stretched; then for some reason she could not help laughing.

'What are you laughing at?' he asked in astonishment.

She did not know what to say. She felt she wanted to kiss Uvar Ivanovich.

'*Flat on his back,*' she said at last.

Uvar Ivanovich did not so much as raise an eyebrow but he continued to look at her in astonishment. She let her hat and cape drop on to him.

'Dear Uvar Ivanovich,' she said, 'I'm so sleepy, so tired,' and, falling into an arm-chair at his side, she began to laugh again.

'Hm,' Uvar Ivanovich grunted sadly, waggling his fingers, 'this is . . . I must say . . . yes . . .'

Elena looked round her. 'I shall have to part from all this soon,' she thought; 'and how strange it is: I don't feel any fear, or doubts, or regrets . . . but no, I am sorry for Mama!' Then the shrine appeared before her eyes again, she heard the sound of his voice, she felt his arms about her. Her heart was glad, but faint; it, too, seemed weary with happiness. She thought of the old beggar-woman; 'It seems as though she really did carry my grief away,' she thought. 'Oh, how happy I am! how undeservedly happy, and how suddenly it has all happened!' If she had only given way just a little, she would have burst into sweet, interminable tears. She could only restrain herself by laughing. Reclining in that chair it seemed to her that whatever attitude she fell into was the most comfortable possible; it was as if she were being rocked to sleep in a cradle. All her movements were slow and gentle; where was the awkwardness and abruptness now? Zoya came into the room: Elena was sure she had never seen a prettier face; Anna Vassilyevna came in: Elena felt a pang, but then how tenderly she kissed her good-natured Mama on the forehead, just below where the hair began to grow, that hair already touched with grey! Then she went to her room, and how everything smiled at her there! With what a feeling of shy triumph and at the same time of humility she sat down on her bed, that same bed on which three hours ago she had passed such moments of bitterness. 'And yet,' she thought, 'even then I knew he loved me, yes, and before then, too . . . but no, no, that's a sinful thought! . . . You are my wife,' she whispered, and covering her face fell on to her knees.

Towards evening she became more serious. The thought that she would not soon see Insarov again depressed her. It was not possible for him to stay with Bersyenev without arousing suspicion, so they had settled on the following plan: Insarov was to return to Moscow, and come and visit them two or three times before the autumn; on her part, she promised to write to him, and if possible appoint a rendezvous somewhere near Kuntsovo. When tea was served she came downstairs to the drawing-room, where she found all the family. Shubin was there too, and he looked at her sharply as soon as she appeared. She would have liked to talk to him in the old friendly way, but she was afraid of his keen insight and of how she herself would react to it. She felt it was not without reason that he had left her in peace for more than two weeks. Soon afterwards Bersyenev arrived; he brought greetings to Anna Vassilyevna from Insarov, who apologized for having returned to Moscow without coming to pay his respects. That was the first time during the day that Elena had heard Insarov's name mentioned and she felt herself flush. She realized that she ought to express regret at the sudden departure of so good a friend; but she was unable to bring herself to practise such deceit, and continued sitting motionless and speechless, while her mother sighed and lamented. Elena tried to stay by Bersyenev; she was not afraid of him, although he did know part of her secret, and under his protection she took refuge from Shubin, who still persisted in looking at her, not mockingly, but searchingly. Bersyenev too grew rather perplexed as the evening passed: he had expected to see her more downcast than she was. Fortunately an argument about art developed between him and Shubin, and she sat aside and listened to their voices as in a dream. Gradually not only they, but the room and everything in it seemed to melt into the dream: the samovar on the table, Uvar Ivanovich's short waistcoat, Zoya's polished finger-nails, the portrait of the Grand Duke Konstantin Pavlovich on the wall, all receded from her, grew misty and ceased to exist. She only felt sorry for them all. 'What have they to live for?' she thought.

'Do you feel sleepy, Lenochka?' her mother asked.

She did not hear her mother's question.

'A half-justified insinuation, you say' – these words, uttered abruptly by Shubin, suddenly aroused her attention. 'But surely,' he continued, 'it's precisely in that sort of remark that the savour, the relish, lies. The justified insinuation induces despondency, it's unchristian – the unjustified insinuation leaves one indifferent, it's just silly; but the half-justified – that's what irritates you and makes you lose patience. For instance, if I said that Elena was in love with one of us, what sort of an insinuation would that be?'

'Oh, Monsieur Paul,' Elena said, 'I wish I could show you how angry you make me – but really, I can't. I'm very tired.'

'Why don't you go and lie down, then?' Anna Vassilyevna said; she always dozed in the evening, and consequently was glad to send the others to bed. 'Come, kiss me and be off with you; Andrei Petrovich will excuse you.'

Elena kissed her mother, bowed to them all and left the room. Shubin walked with her to the door.

'Elena Nikolayevna,' he whispered to her in the doorway, 'you may trample on Monsieur Paul, you may trample on him without mercy, yet Monsieur Paul blesses you and blesses your little feet too, and the shoes that they wear, and the soles of your shoes.'

Elena shrugged her shoulders; reluctantly she gave him her hand – not the hand that Insarov had kissed – and returning to her room, undressed at once, lay down and went to sleep. It was a deep, untroubled sleep, such as even children do not know; she slept as only a baby sleeps when, recovering from a sickness, its mother sits by its cot, gazes at it and listens to its quiet breathing.

XX

'COME to my room for a moment,' Shubin said to Bersyenev, as soon as his friend had taken leave of Anna Vassilyevna, 'I've got something to show you.'

Bersyenev went with him into the wing of the house. He was astonished to see all the statuettes, busts and unfinished studies which, wrapped round in pieces of damp cloth, occupied every corner of the room.

'I see you've been doing a lot of work,' he commented.

'You have to do something,' Shubin answered. 'If you're unlucky with one thing, you have to try something else. However, I'm like a Corsican, I'm more concerned with my vendetta than with pure art. *Trema, Bisanzia!*'

'I don't understand you,' Bersyenev said.

'Just wait and you'll see. Be good enough to look at this, my worthy friend and patron – my Revenge Number One.'

Shubin unwrapped one of the pieces and Bersyenev saw an excellent and wonderfully life-like bust of Insarov. Shubin had captured the features accurately to the smallest detail; there was an expression of nobility about the face, of honesty, magnanimity and courage. Bersyenev was enraptured.

'But that's quite delightful!' he exclaimed. 'I congratulate you. It's good enough for exhibition! Why do you call this magnificent work "Revenge"?'

'Because, sir, I intend to present this magnificent work, as you are pleased to call it, to Elena Nikolayevna on her name-day. You observe the allegory? ... We are not blind, we perceive what's going on around us, but at the same time we are gentlemen, my dear sir, and we revenge ourselves à la gentleman.'

'And look here,' Shubin added, unwrapping another small statue; 'seeing that the artist (according to the latest aesthetic principles) enjoys the enviable right of embodying in himself every sort of beastliness, and of transmuting this beastliness into some creative masterpiece, we, in creating this masterpiece Number Two, have taken our revenge not by any means à la gentleman, but simply en canaille.'

He deftly pulled off the cloth, and presented to Bersyenev's gaze a statuette done in the *Dantan* manner, again depicting Insarov. Anything more wittily malicious it would have been difficult to conceive. The young Bulgarian was represented as a ram rearing up on its hind legs with its horns down, ready to butt. So much stupid self-importance and hot-headedness, so much clumsy obstinacy and narrow-mindedness were expressed in the face of this 'consort of the fine-fleeced ewes', and at the same time the likeness was so striking and unmistakable, that Bersyenev could not help bursting into laughter.

'Well? Does it amuse you?' Shubin asked. 'You recognize the hero? Do you advise me to exhibit this one too? I propose, sir, to present this one to myself on my own name-day ... Your Excellency, permit me to show you a little trick!'

And Shubin skipped into the air two or three times, kicking himself on the back with the soles of his feet.

Bersyenev picked up the cloth and threw it over the statuette.

'Oh, you big-hearted ...' Shubin began: 'now, what

famous man was known for his bigness-of-heart? Never
mind. And now,' he went on, solemnly and tragically unwrapping a third, rather larger lump of clay, 'you are
about to see something which will demonstrate to you the
wise humility and the perspicacity of your friend. This
will convince you that he, the pure artist once again, feels
the desirability and usefulness of slapping himself in the
face. Behold!'

He pulled off the cloth and Bersyenev saw two heads set
side by side in close proximity, as though they had grown
together. At first he could not make out what they were,
but on looking more closely he saw that one represented
Annushka, the other Shubin himself; in fact, they were
more like caricatures than serious portraits. Annushka was
depicted as a handsome, gross wench, with a low forehead,
eyes deep-set in fat, and a pertly up-turned nose. Her
coarse lips grinned insolently and the whole face expressed
sensuality and a careless audacity, though it was not ill-
natured. Shubin had represented himself as an emaciated
roué with sunken cheeks; thin strands of hair hung im-
potently down, there was a vacant expression in the lifeless
eyes, and his nose was sharply pointed, like the nose of a
corpse.

Bersyenev turned away in revulsion.

'A nice couple, eh?' Shubin remarked – 'I wish you'd
compose a suitable inscription for it; I've thought of in-
scriptions for the first two. Under the bust I shall put:
"Hero, resolved to save his country"; and under the
statuette: "Sausage-manufacturers beware!" But as for
this – well, what do you say – "The destiny of Pavel
Yakovlevich Shubin, artist!" . . . Will that do?'

'Stop!' Bersyenev retorted. 'Why waste time on
such . . .' He could not find the right word.

143

'You mean filth? No, my friend, I'm sorry, but if anything goes to the show, it's this group.'

'Filth is the word,' Bersyenev said. 'But really, what is this nonsense about? There's not a trace of that sort of development in you, though up to the present our artists have been richly endowed in that respect, unfortunately. You've simply libelled yourself.'

'You think so?' Shubin said gloomily. 'If I've escaped it so far and if I fall a victim to it in the future, then it will be a certain person that's responsible. Do you know,' he added, frowning tragically, 'that I've already tried drink?'

'It's not true!'

'It's true, I tell you,' Shubin retorted, and then he grinned and his face lightened; 'but I don't like it, old man, it sticks in my throat and afterwards my head feels like a big drum. The great Lushchihin himself – Harlampi Lushchihin – the man with the greatest thirst in Moscow, and some say in all Russia – he says I'll never be any good at it. The bottle has nothing to say to me, according to him.'

Bersyenev made as if to knock down the offending group, but Shubin stopped him.

'No, leave it alone,' he said, 'it will serve as a horrid warning, a scarecrow.'

Bersyenev laughed.

'Very well, then, I'll spare your scarecrow,' he said. 'Here's to Art, pure and eternal!'

'To Art!' Shubin joined in, 'Art which adds lustre to the good and takes the sting out of evil!'

The friends shook hands warmly and parted.

XXI

ELENA'S first emotion on waking up was of happy consternation. 'Can it be true, can it be true?' she asked herself, and her heart grew faint with happiness. Memories flooded over her, submerged her and then again that blissful, rapturous peace descended on her. But as the morning passed she grew a little restless and during the ensuing days she began to feel listless and dispirited. True, she now knew what she really wanted, but that did not make things easier for her. That never-to-be-forgotten meeting had violently changed the routine of her life for all time, her old existence seemed remote from her now – yet all the while everything around went on as usual, everything took its normal course, as though nothing had changed, and Elena's participation and co-operation was expected as before. She tried to start a letter to Insarov, but even that failed; on paper the words appeared either lifeless or false. She had finished her diary, and drawn a thick line under the last sentence; that was the past, and now all her thoughts and feelings were in the future. It was a distressing time for her: to sit with her mother, who suspected nothing, to listen to her and talk to her, seemed somehow criminal, and she felt there was something false inside her; though she had nothing to be ashamed of, she felt revolted at herself; often she experienced an almost irresistible desire to tell everything without concealment, come what might. 'Why,' she thought, 'why didn't Dmitri take me away from the shrine there and then, wherever he wanted to go?

Didn't he say I was his wife before God? Why am I here?' Suddenly she began to shun everyone – even Uvar Ivanovich, who waggled his fingers and was more perplexed than ever. The things and people about her no longer seemed kind and affectionate, even that dream-like quality was gone: they weighed on her persistently, like some ghastly nightmarish burden; they seemed to reproach her, to upbraid her, to be unwilling to understand her . . . 'You still belong to us,' they seemed to say. Even her poor little foster-children, the down-trodden birds and animals, looked at her – at least, it seemed so to her – with suspicion and hostility. She began to be conscience-stricken and ashamed of her own feelings. 'After all, this is my home, isn't it?' she thought. 'This is my family and my country?' But another voice answered persistently: 'No, it's no longer your family or your country.' Fear overcame her, and she was angry; at her own faint-heartedness . . . Her troubles were only just beginning and already she was losing patience – was this what she had promised him?

She did not regain her self-possession quickly, but as one week passed and then another she grew a little calmer and accustomed herself to the new situation. She wrote two short notes to Insarov, and took them to the post herself; she could not, for shame and pride, bring herself to entrust them to the maid. She was already beginning to expect Insarov to visit her. . . . But, instead of him, one lovely sunny morning, Nikolai Artyomevich arrived.

XXII

No one in the Stahov household had ever seen the retired
lieutenant of the guards in so sour a mood and at the same
time so full of self-assurance and his own importance as he
was on that day. He came into the drawing-room in his
coat and hat, walking slowly with his legs wide apart and
stamping his heels on the floor. Going up to the mirror he
gazed at himself intently, biting his lips and wagging his
head with calm severity. Anna Vassilyevna met him with
outward excitement and secret pleasure (she invariably felt
the same way when she met him); he did not even greet
her or take off his hat, but silently stretched out his hand for
Elena to kiss his chamois leather glove. Anna Vassilyevna
began to question him about his course of treatment – he
did not reply; Uvar Ivanovich came in – he glanced at him
and said: 'Ba.' He was usually cold and patronizing with
Uvar Ivanovich, though he recognized in him 'traces of the
genuine Stahov blood'. Most good Russian families, of
course, are convinced of the existence of special charac-
teristics of their breed which are possessed by them alone;
one not infrequently hears talk *entre nous* of the 'such-and-
such nose' or the 'such-and-such neck'. Zoya came into
the room and curtsied to Nikolai Artyomevich. He
grunted, sat down in an arm-chair, demanded coffee and
only then took off his hat. The coffee was brought and he
drank a cup; then looking at each in turn he growled:
'Kindly leave the room' – adding, as he turned to his wife:
'*Et vous, madame, restez, je vous prie.*'

All left the room except Anna Vassilyevna, who was trembling with emotion. The solemnity of Nikolai Artyomevich's behaviour had impressed her deeply, and she expected to hear something extraordinary.

'What is it?' she exclaimed, as soon as the door was closed.

He glanced at her indifferently.

'Nothing in particular,' he said; 'but where did you get this habit of suddenly assuming the air of a victim going to the sacrifice?' At each word he turned down the corners of his mouth for no apparent reason. 'I only wanted to warn you that we should be having a visitor to dinner today.'

'Who then?'

'Mr Kurnatovski, Yegor Andreyevich Kurnatovski. You don't know him; he's a chief secretary at the Senate.'

'He's coming to dinner today?'

'Yes.'

'And you ordered everyone out of the room just to tell me that?'

Nikolai Artyomevich again glanced at his wife, this time ironically.

'Does that surprise you? You must wait for the surprise.'

He paused, and Anna Vassilyevna said nothing for a moment.

'I would like . . .' she began.

'I know you always regard me as an immoral person,' Nikolai Artyomevich observed suddenly.

'I!' exclaimed Anna Vassilyevna, with astonishment.

'And maybe you're right, too. I don't deny that I have on occasion given you just cause for dissatisfaction' – ('my grey horses' flashed through her mind) – 'though you yourself will agree that in your state of health, as you know . . .'

'But I don't blame you in the least, Nikolai Artyomevich.'

'*C'est possible*. In any case, I don't propose to justify myself. Time will justify me. But I feel obliged to inform you that I am aware of my duty and I know how to safeguard the interests of the family which . . . has been entrusted to my care.'

'Whatever does this mean?' thought Anna Vassilyevna. (She little knew that on the previous evening, in a corner of the lounge at the English Club, there had been an argument about the inability of the Russian to make an effective speech. 'Who among us knows how to speak?' someone had exclaimed: 'Mention anyone.' – 'Well, there's Stahov, for example,' said another, pointing to Nikolai Artyomevich, who happened to be standing by; and Nikolai Artyomevich had almost crowed with delight.)

'For instance,' he went on, 'there's our daughter Elena. Don't you consider it's high time she took a resolute step along the path to . . . to get married, I mean? All this philosophy and philanthropy is well enough up to a certain point, up to a certain age. It's time for her to stop her vapourings and quit the society of all these artists, scholars and Montenegrins, and become like other people.'

'What am I to understand by this?' Anna Vassilyevna asked.

'Just this – if you'll be good enough to listen,' Nikolai Artyomevich answered, still turning down the corners of his mouth all the while. 'I will speak plainly and without beating about the bush: I have made the acquaintance of this young Mr Kurnatovski; I have made a friend of him, in the hope that he may become my son-in-law. I venture

149

to think that, having seen him, you won't accuse me of undue partiality or rashness of judgement.' (Nikolai Artyomevich was admiring his own eloquence as he spoke.) 'He is a lawyer, a man of excellent education, with delightful manners: thirty-three years of age, a chief secretary and collegiate councillor, with the Order of Stanislav. You will grant, I hope, that I am not among those *pères de comédie* who get excited about a man's rank; but you yourself have told me that Elena Nikolayevna likes sensible, steady people, and Yegor Andreyevich is first of all a business man. However, just at the moment our daughter is more impressed by generous conduct: so I would have you know that Yegor Andreyevich, as soon as it became possible – that is, possible to exist in comfort on his own income – at once renounced the allowance which his father made to him, in favour of his brothers.'

'And who is his father?' Anna Vassilyevna asked.

'His father? He, too, is well known in his own sphere, a person of the highest principles, *un vrai stoïcien*; he is a retired major, I believe, and manages all the estates of the Counts B . . .'

'Oh!' Anna Vassilyevna said.

'Oh! Why "Oh!"?' Nikolai Artyomevich retorted. 'Can it be that you also are tainted with prejudice?'

'But I didn't say anything,' Anna Vassilyevna was beginning . . .

'But you said "Oh!" . . . However that may be, I deemed it necessary to let you know the trend of my thoughts – and I venture to think . . . to hope that Mr Kurnatovski will be welcomed here with open arms. This is none of your Montenegrins.'

'Of course. I shall merely have to send for Vanka the cook and tell him to prepare a little extra.'

'You won't expect me to concern myself with that,' Nikolai Artyomevich said; and getting up, he put on his hat and set off for a stroll in the garden, whistling as he went. (Someone had told him that whistling was only permissible when at home in the country or at the riding school.) Shubin watched him from the window of his room and silently put out his tongue.

At ten minutes to four an open carriage drew up at the porch of the Stahov villa and a man of pleasing appearance, still young, and simply and elegantly attired, stepped out and sent in his name. Yegor Andreyevich Kurnatovski had arrived.

This is what, among other things, Elena wrote to Insarov on the following day:

'You must congratulate me, dearest Dmitri; I have a suitor. He came to dinner yesterday: I think Papa got to know him in the English Club and invited him here. Of course, he didn't come as a suitor yesterday: but kind little Mama, to whom Papa had confided his hopes, whispered to me what sort of a guest he was. His name is Yegor Andreyevich Kurnatovski, and he is a chief secretary at the Senate. First let me tell you what he looks like. He is not very tall – shorter than you – and well-built; he has regular features; his hair is cut short and he has long side-whiskers. His sharp brown eyes are rather small (like yours), his lips are wide but not full. In his eyes and on his lips there is an official sort of smile, which seems to be perpetually *on duty*. He behaves very simply and unaffectedly, he talks precisely and everything about him is precise. He walks, laughs and eats as though it were all a matter of business. "How she has studied him!" you'll be thinking, I dare say. Yes, I have – in order to describe him to you: and anyway, shouldn't I study the gentleman who is courting me?

There's something very strong-willed about him – and dull and empty at the same time – and honest, too: they say that he is in fact a very honest man. You are strong-willed also, my dear – but in a different sort of way from him. At dinner he sat next to me and Shubin sat opposite. At first the conversation was about business; they say that he understands these things very well, and almost gave up his official post to manage a big factory. It's a pity he didn't! Then Shubin began to talk about the theatre. Mr Kurnatovski announced – without false modesty, I must admit – that he knew nothing about art. That reminded me of you – but then I thought to myself: no, it's in a different way that Dmitri and I don't understand art. What Kurnatovski seemed to imply was: I don't understand art, and what's more art isn't necessary, though in a well-ordered state it's allowed to exist. Incidentally, he seemed rather unimpressed by Petersburg life and polite society: once he even called himself a proletarian. "We're labouring folk," he said. I thought that if my Dmitri had said that I wouldn't have liked it at all, but as for this fellow – well, let him talk and brag! With me he was very civil, but it seemed to me that he talked to me all the time in a very, very condescending and superior way. When he wants to praise anyone, he says that "So-and-so has *principles*" – that's his favourite word. I think he's confident and industrious and capable of self-sacrifice (you see how impartial I am) – that is, of sacrificing his own interests, but he's a great despot at the same time. I'd pity anyone who fell into his hands! At dinner they began to discuss bribery . . .

"'I can appreciate," he said, "that in many cases a man who takes bribes may not be culpable, that he couldn't have done otherwise in any case; nevertheless, if he's found out he should be exterminated."

'"Exterminate someone who isn't guilty!" I cried.

'"Yes, on principle."

'"What principle?" Shubin asked.

'Kurnatovski was taken aback and said:

'"There's surely no need to explain that."

'Papa, who seems to think very highly of him, chimed in that of course there wasn't – and that cut short the conversation, to my annoyance. In the evening Bersyenev came and got into a terrific argument with him: I've never seen our good Andrei Petrovich so excited. Mr Kurnatovski in no way denied the value of science and the universities and so on ... but at the same time I could understand Bersyenev's indignation. Kurnatovski seems to regard all that as a sort of intellectual gymnastics. Shubin came to me after dinner and said: "Now just compare this fellow with someone else we know (he can't bring himself to say your name) – they are both practical men, but you see what a difference there is: in one case there's a genuine, living ideal inspired by life itself – whereas here there's not even a sense of duty, but simply an official honesty and superficial, practical ability" ... Shubin is clever, and I remembered what he said so that I could tell you: but as for me, I see nothing in common between you. You have *faith*, and he hasn't, because you can't call faith what is merely a belief in yourself alone.

'He went away late, but Mama managed to tell me that he liked me, and that Papa was in raptures ... I wonder if he told them that I had principles? I almost said to Mama that I was very sorry, but I already had a husband. Why is it Papa dislikes you so? With Mama we should manage somehow ...

'Oh, my darling! The reason I've described this gentleman in so much detail to you is just to stifle my own

153

longings. I don't seem to live without you, I see you and hear you all the time . . . I'm waiting for you, only not here at home as you suggested – imagine how difficult and awkward it would be for us – but you know, where I told you in my letter – in that wood . . . Oh, my darling, how I love you!'

XXIII

ABOUT three weeks after Kurnatovski's first visit, Anna Vassilyevna, to Elena's great joy, returned to her house in Moscow. It was a large, two-storied, wooden house, near the Prechistenka, a house with columns and white plaster lyres and garlands above each window; it had a small front garden, a huge grass-grown courtyard surrounded by out-buildings, and a well in the courtyard with a dog kennel by its side. Anna Vassilyevna had never left the country so early, but this year, with the first approach of the cold autumn weather, her gumboils began to 'plague' her; Nikolai Artyomevich, for his part, had finished his treatment and was anxious for his wife's return – the more so as Avgustina Christianovna had gone to visit her cousin in Reval; then a foreign family had arrived in Moscow and was giving exhibitions of 'plastic poses', *des poses plastiques*, and the account of these in the *Moscow Journal* had powerfully stimulated Anna Vassilyevna's curiosity. In short, a longer stay in the country had seemed inconvenient and, according to Nikolai Artyomevich, actually incompatible with the 'fulfilment of his plans'. The last two weeks at the villa had seemed very long to Elena. Kurnatovski had visited them twice, on Sundays; on other days he was too busy. He really came to see Elena, but he talked more to Zoya, who liked him very much. '*Das ist ein Mann!*' she would think, looking at his dark, manly countenance and listening to his self-confident, condescending talk. She felt that no one had such a wonderful voice as he had, no one could say with such distinction: 'I have the honour,' or 'Delighted, I'm sure.' Insarov did not visit the Stahovs, but Elena saw him once clandestinely at a rendezvous in a small wood by the Moscow River; even then they had only managed to exchange a few words. Shubin returned to Moscow with Anna Vassilyevna; Bersyenev came back a few days later.

One day shortly after their return, Insarov was sitting in his room, re-reading for the third time the letters which had been brought to him from Bulgaria by messenger; it had not been safe to send them by post. He was much disturbed by them. Events in the Balkans were developing rapidly; the occupation of the Principalities by Russian troops had caused general excitement; the storm was rising, the breath of imminent, inevitable war was in the air; conflagration was breaking out all round and no one could tell where it would spread or when it would stop; all the old resentments, and long-cherished hopes were awakening – everything was astir. Insarov's heart was stirred also: his hopes too were coming true. 'But isn't it too early, won't it all be useless?' he thought, clenching his fist. 'We aren't ready yet – however, so be it. I shall have to go.'

There was a faint sound at the door; it opened quickly, and Elena entered.

Insarov trembled, flung himself towards her, fell on his knees, and, with his arms round her waist, pressed his head against her.

'You didn't expect me?' she said, panting. (She had run up the stairs quickly.) 'Darling, darling!' She laid both hands on his head and looked round. 'So this is where you live. I found you quite easily: your landlord's daughter brought me. We've been back three days ... I meant to

156

write to you, but I thought it would be better to come myself. I can only stay with you for a quarter of an hour: get up and lock the door.'

He stood up, bolted the door, then returned and took her hands in his. He could not speak, his joy seemed to have taken his breath away. Smiling, she looked into his eyes . . . there was so much happiness in them . . . Suddenly she felt embarrassed.

'Wait,' she said, gently withdrawing her hands, 'let me take off my hat.'

She undid the ribbons of her hat, and flung it aside, slipped her cape from her shoulders, put her hair straight; then she sat down on the old sofa. Insarov watched her motionless, as if fascinated.

'Do sit down,' she said, without looking up at him, and pointing to the seat by her side.

Insarov sat down, not on the sofa, but on the floor at her feet.

'Now take my gloves off,' she said unsteadily. She was beginning to feel frightened.

He unbuttoned one glove and half pulled it off; then he pressed his lips passionately to the pale, soft, slender hand beneath it.

She trembled and tried to prevent him with the other hand: he began to kiss the other hand. She pulled it away from him; he flung back his head, she looked into his face, and bent down . . . their lips met . . .

A moment passed; she broke away, and stood up whispering 'No, no'; then quickly went over to the writing-table.

'I'm the lady of the house here,' she said, 'you mustn't have any secrets from me.' Trying to appear unconcerned, she turned her back on him. 'What a lot of papers,' she said; 'what are these letters?'

Insarov frowned.

'Those letters?' he said, getting up from the floor. 'You can read them.'

Elena turned them over in her hands.

'There are so many of them and the writing's so small – and I must be going in a minute . . . I won't bother with them! I suppose they're not from a rival? . . . And they're not even in Russian,' she added, fingering the thin sheets of paper.

Insarov went up to her and gently put his arm round her waist. She turned to him suddenly, smiled happily and leaned on his shoulder.

'Those letters are from Bulgaria, Elena; my friends have written to me, they want me to go.'

'To go to Bulgaria now?'

'Yes, now. While there's still time, and it's still possible to get through.'

She suddenly threw her arms round his neck.

'You'll take me with you, won't you?' she said. He pressed her to him.

'Oh, my darling girl, my own heroine, how bravely you said that! But wouldn't it be wickedness and madness to take you with me – me, with no home or family! And think where to . . .'

She put her hand over his mouth.

'Hush . . . or I'll get cross and never come and see you again. Isn't everything decided, isn't everything settled between us? Am I not your wife? Do wives part from their husbands?'

'Wives don't go to war,' he said, with a wry smile.

'No, not when they can stay behind. But how can I stay here?'

'Elena, you're an angel! . . . But just consider, I may have to leave Moscow in a fortnight. There's no longer any question of continuing with my lectures, or finishing my work here.'

'What of it, if you do have to go soon?' Elena interrupted. 'If you want me to, I'll stay here now, yes now, I'll stay with you for ever and not go home, if you want it. Shall we go at once?'

Insarov pressed her to him with redoubled fervour.

'God punish me if I'm doing wrong!' he exclaimed. 'From this day we belong to one another for ever!'

'Shall I stay?' Elena asked.

'No, my pure heart, my treasure. You must go home today, but be ready. This isn't a matter we can settle at once; we must think it all out carefully. We shall need money and a passport . . .'

'I've got money,' Elena interrupted; 'eighty roubles.'

'It isn't a lot,' Insarov said. 'Still, it will help.'

'I can get some more, I can borrow, I can ask Mama . . . No, I won't ask her . . . But I can sell my watch . . . I've ear-rings and two bracelets . . . and some lace.'

'It's not a question of money, Elena. It's the passport, your passport – how shall we manage that?'

'Yes . . . how shall we manage that? Is a passport absolutely necessary?'

'Absolutely.'

Elena smiled.

'I've just thought of something, Dmitri. It was when I was still a child, I remember . . . We had a maid who ran away. She was caught and forgiven, and she lived with us a long time afterwards . . . yet she was always called "Tatyana the Fugitive". I little thought then that I might be a fugitive some day, like her.'

'Elena, aren't you ashamed of yourself?'

159

'But why? Of course, it's better to go with a passport if you can – but if you can't –'

'We'll settle all that later on, later on,' Insarov said; 'you must wait, just give me time to look round, to think things out. We must discuss things together thoroughly later on. As for money, I have some too.'

Elena brushed aside the hair which had fallen on to his forehead.

'Oh, Dmitri! Won't it be wonderful, travelling together!'

'Yes,' Insarov said; 'but, when we arrive . . .'

'Well, what?' Elena interrupted. 'Isn't it wonderful to die together too? But why should we die? We're young, we're going to live. How old are you? Twenty–six?'

'Twenty-six.'

'I'm twenty . . . there's plenty of time ahead of us. And to think you wanted to run away from me! You didn't need any Russian love, did you, Bulgarian? We shall just see how you get rid of me now. But what would have happened to us, if I hadn't come to see you that time?'

'You know what forced me to go away, Elena.'

'I know: you fell in love, and you were afraid. But did you really not suspect that someone might have fallen in love with you?'

'Upon my word I didn't, Elena.'

She kissed him quickly, unexpectedly.

'That's just the reason I love you so. And now good-bye.'

'Can't you stay longer?' Insarov asked.

'No, darling. Do you think it was easy for me to get away by myself? A quarter of an hour's been gone a long time.' She put on her cape and hat. 'You must come and see us tomorrow evening – no, the day after tomorrow.

It will be difficult and boring, but it can't be helped: at least we shall see one another. Good-bye now. Let me out.' He embraced her for the last time. 'Oh, look, you've broken my watch-chain, my clumsy one! Never mind, it's all the better: I'll go home by Kuznetski Bridge and leave it there to be mended. If anybody asks where I was, I shall say I was at Kuznetski Bridge.' She took hold of the door-handle. 'By the way, I forgot to tell you: Monsieur Kurnatovski will probably offer me his hand in a day or two . . . and I shall offer him this –' She put her thumb to her nose and wagged her fingers in the air. 'Good-bye: *au revoir*. I know the way now – and you mustn't lose any time.'

Elena opened the door slightly, listened, turned to Insarov and nodded, then slipped out of the room.

For a moment Insarov stood in front of the closed door and also listened. He heard the door into the yard bang downstairs, then went to the sofa and sat down, covering his eyes with his hand. Nothing like this had ever happened to him before. 'What have I done to deserve such love?' he thought. 'Am I dreaming?'

But the faint odour of mignonette which Elena had brought into his mean, dark room reminded him of her presence. With it, there still seemed to linger in the air the sound of that young voice and those light footsteps, and the warmth and freshness of that virginal young body.

XXIV

INSAROV decided to await more positive news from Bulgaria, but he began to make preparations for his departure. It was a very difficult situation. In his own case there were no obstacles in the way – he had merely to ask for a passport; but what was to be done for Elena? To obtain a passport for her by legitimate means was impossible. To get married secretly and then to go and announce it to her parents . . . ? 'Then they would let us go,' he thought. 'But if they didn't? Then we'd go in any case . . . But suppose they made a complaint . . . suppose they . . . No, it's better to try and get a passport somehow or other.'

He decided to take advice (without mentioning names, of course) from an acquaintance of his, a certain retired, or possibly discharged, public prosecutor, who was old and experienced in every sort of clandestine undertaking. This worthy gentleman lived some distance away, and Insarov had to drive for a whole hour in a wretched little open cab – only to find that he was not at home; and on the return journey he got soaked to the skin in a heavy downpour which came on suddenly. The next morning, in spite of a rather severe headache, he set off once more. The retired prosecutor listened to him attentively, looking at him sideways with his small, sly, tobacco-coloured eyes, and taking snuff all the while from a snuff-box which was embellished with a picture of a full-bosomed nymph. Having heard him out, he asked for 'more precision in his

exposition of the facts of the case'; and seeing that Insarov –
who had, after all, only approached him reluctantly – was
unwilling to enter into details, confined himself to advising
him to arm himself well with money; then he asked him
to call again another time – 'when you are more trustful
and less suspicious,' he added, taking a pinch of snuff over
the open box. 'As for the passport,' he went on, as though
to himself, 'that's not a matter beyond the power of man
to arrange; if you're travelling, for instance, who is to know
whether you are Marya Bredihina or Karolina Vogelmeier?' Insarov was conscious of a feeling of revulsion, but
he thanked the old man and promised to call back in a few
days.

That evening he went to the Stahovs'. Anna Vassilyevna
welcomed him affectionately, reproaching him for having
quite forgotten them; she thought he looked pale and
inquired after his health. Nikolai Artyomevich did not
say a word, merely glancing at him with a sort of distrait,
brooding curiosity, and Shubin's attitude was cold; but
Elena's behaviour astonished him. She was expecting him,
and had put on the same dress that she had worn on the
day of their first meeting in the shrine; but she greeted him
so calmly, she was so gracious, gay and unconcerned that
no one, looking at her, would have guessed that the fate
of this girl was already decided, that the animation of her
features and the lightness and charm of all her movements
were due only to the secret consciousness of requited love.
She poured out tea instead of Zoya, joking and chattering
all the while. She knew that Shubin would be watching her
and that Insarov would be incapable of disguising his feelings and shamming indifference, so she was taking pre-
cautions in advance. She was not mistaken; Shubin's eyes
never left her, and Insarov was very taciturn and gloomy

all the evening. Elena was so happy that she felt she wanted to tease him.

'Well,' she asked suddenly, 'how's the plan going?'

Insarov looked embarrassed.

'What plan?' he asked.

'Have you forgotten?' she answered, looking into his face and laughing – and only Insarov knew the significance of that happy laugh. 'Your Bulgarian reader for Russians?'

'*Quelle bourde!*' muttered Nikolai Artyomevich contemptuously.

Zoya sat down at the piano. Elena gave a scarcely perceptible shrug of the shoulders and glanced at the door, as if to tell Insarov to go home. Then she slowly tapped on the table twice and looked at him. He understood that he was to see her again in two days' time, and she smiled quickly as she saw that he understood. He got up and began to take his leave – he was feeling unwell. Then Kurnatovski appeared. Nikolai Artyomevich jumped up, raised his right hand high into the air and let it fall gently on to that of the chief secretary. Insarov stayed for a few minutes in order to have a look at his rival. Elena shook her head at him slyly – and her father not deeming it necessary to introduce him to the new guest, Insarov departed, exchanging a last glance with Elena as he went. Shubin pondered and pondered – then fell into a furious argument with Kurnatovski on some legal question, about which he knew nothing.

Insarov did not sleep all night and felt ill the next morning. He got up and began to put his papers into order and write some letters, though his head was heavy and muddled. By dinner-time he was feverish and he could eat nothing; by evening the fever had increased greatly, there were pains in his limbs and his head ached violently. He lay down on the sofa, the sofa on which Elena had been sitting so recently. 'This serves me right,' he thought, 'for going out to see that old swindler,' and he tried to sleep. But the fever already had him in its grip; his head throbbed madly, his blood seemed to be aflame, his thoughts were whirling round like birds in the air. He lost consciousness ... He lay prostrate on his back, and suddenly it seemed to him that someone was standing over him and quietly laughing and whispering. He opened his eyes with an effort and the light from the guttering candle cut through him like a knife – in front of him he saw the old prosecutor, wearing a dressing-gown and a silk scarf round the waist, just as he had seen him the previous evening. 'Karolina Vogelmeier,' the toothless mouth was mumbling. Insarov looked at him, but the old man began to broaden out, to expand and grow until he was no longer a man but a tree ... and now Insarov was having to climb the steep branches; he clutched at them in vain and fell on to a sharp stone, hurting his chest ... he saw Karolina Vogelmeier squatting there like a street-hawker and jabbering away: 'Cakes and pies, cakes and pies!' ... he saw blood flowing and swords flashing with unbearable brilliance ... he saw Elena, and everything vanished in a blood-red chaos.

XXV

'SOME fellow has called and wants to see you,' Bersyenev's servant informed him on the evening of the following day.

'Goodness knows who he is – a locksmith or some such person.' This servant was remarkable for his stern bearing towards his master and his sceptical attitude of mind.

'Ask him in,' Bersyenev said.

The 'locksmith' entered. Bersyenev recognized the tailor who kept Insarov's lodging.

'What do you want?' Bersyenev asked.

'I've come to see Your Honour,' the tailor began, slowly shuffling from one foot to the other, and now and then waving his right hand in the air and gripping his cuff with three fingers; 'our lodger, he's terribly ill, my word he is.'

'Insarov?'

'Yes, him, our lodger, yesterday morning he was still all right – but in the evening he only asked for a drink, and my missis took him some water. Then in the night he began to jabber, we could hear him because there's only a thin wall, you see. And this morning he can't talk and he's lying there like a log and my God what a fever he's in! I thought to myself, my word, he might go and die, I must tell the police, I thought. Because he's all by himself, you see; but my missis said to me: "Slip round to that gentleman, the one he took a room with in the country, perhaps he'll tell you something, he might come himself." So I've come to Your Honour, you see, we can't, I mean . . .'

Bersyenev snatched his cap, thrust a rouble into the

tailor's hand and at once hurried round with him to Insarov's lodging.

He found him lying unconscious on the sofa, still in his
clothes. His face was terribly altered. Bersyenev told them
to undress him at once and move him to the bed, and then
dashed out to fetch a doctor ... The doctor prescribed
leeches, plasters, calomel and blood-letting.

'Is he dangerously ill?' Bersyenev asked.

'Yes, very,' the doctor answered, 'there's severe in-
flammation of the lungs; pneumonia is developing rapidly
and the brain may be affected, but the patient is young. Yet
his very strength is against him in this malady. You sent
for us too late, but nevertheless we shall do everything that
science calls for.'

The doctor was still young himself and had faith in
science.

Bersyenev stayed the night. The landlord and his wife
turned out to be kind and indeed capable people as soon as
they found someone to tell them what to do. At last the
doctor's assistant arrived and began to inflict his treatment
on the patient.

Towards morning Insarov came to for a few minutes
and, on recognizing Bersyenev, asked: 'Am I not well,
then?' He looked round him with the dull, lifeless per-
plexity of a very sick man and again relapsed into uncon-
sciousness. Bersyenev went home and changed his clothes,
collected some books and returned to Insarov's lodging.
He had decided to stay with him, at least for the time
being. He put a screen round the bed and arranged a place
for himself beside the sofa. The day passed slowly and
drearily; Bersyenev only went away in order to have his
meal. Evening came on; he lit a shaded candle and started
to read. All around it was quiet. Occasionally a whisper, a

sigh or a yawn would come from the landlord's room behind the partition; once someone sneezed and was rebuked in a whisper. From Insarov's bed came the sound of heavy and uneven breathing, sometimes broken by a short moan and the uneasy tossing of the sick man's head on the pillow. Strange thoughts flitted through Bersyenev's mind. Here he was in the room of the man whom he knew Elena loved, and that man's life was hanging by a thread . . . He recalled that night when Shubin overtook him and informed him that *he* was the one she loved! But now . . . 'What am I to do now?' he asked himself. Should he let her know about Insarov's illness or should he wait? This would be a sadder story than the one he had had to tell her before; strange, how fate always made him their go-between . . . He decided to wait. His eyes fell on the table, covered with piles of papers. 'Will he be able to fulfil his plans?' Bersyenev thought, 'or must everything go?' He began to pity that young, failing life and vowed to save it . . .

It was a bad night; Insarov was very delirious. Several times Bersyenev got up from the sofa, went on tiptoe to the bed and listened sadly to the sick man's incoherent babbling. Only once he spoke with sudden clarity: 'I don't want it, I don't want it, you mustn't, darling . . .' Bersyenev started and looked at Insarov: his deathly-pale and suffering face was quite still, his arms lay powerless at his side . . . 'I don't want it,' he repeated, almost inaudibly.

The doctor came in the morning, shook his head and prescribed some new medicine.

'He's still far from the crisis,' he said, putting on his hat.

'And after the crisis?' Bersyenev asked.

'After the crisis? There are just two possibilities: *aut Caesar, aut nihil.*' The doctor left, and Bersyenev went out into the street for a while: he felt he needed fresh air. Then he returned and took up a book; he had long since finished with Raumer and he now was studying Grote.

The door creaked quietly and the head of the landlord's daughter, wrapped round as usual with a thick shawl, cautiously appeared through the crack.

'Here's that young lady again,' she said in a whisper, 'the one that gave me sixpence before.'

The head vanished suddenly, and Elena appeared in its place.

Bersyenev jumped up as if something had stung him; but Elena stood motionless and did not utter a sound . . . she seemed to have understood everything in a flash. Dreadfully pale, she went to the screen and looked behind it; she threw up her hands and seemed to turn to stone. Another moment and she would have flung herself on Insarov, but Bersyenev prevented her.

'What are you doing?' he whispered unsteadily, 'you might kill him.'

She staggered back; he led her to the sofa and made her sit down. She glanced at his face, looked him over quickly, then stared at the floor.

'Is he dying?' she asked, so coldly and calmly that he was afraid.

'For God's sake, Elena Nikolayevna,' he said, 'what are you saying? He's ill, yes . . . rather gravely ill; but we shall save him, I'll promise you that.'

'Is he unconscious?' she asked, in the same tone as before.

'Yes, he's unconscious now – it always happens at the beginning of this illness, but it means nothing, nothing – I assure you of that. Take a drink of water.'

She looked up, and he realized that she had not heard him.

'If he dies,' she said, still in the same cold way, 'I shall die, too.'

At that moment Insarov moaned faintly; she trembled, gripped her head in her hands, then began to untie the ribbons of her hat.

'What are you doing?' Bersyenev asked her.

She did not reply.

'What are you doing?' he repeated.

'I'm going to stay here.'

'How do you mean . . . for long?'

'I don't know . . . maybe all day, all night, for ever . . . I don't know.'

'For God's sake, Elena Nikolayevna, come to your senses. Naturally, I didn't expect to see you here at all – but in any case I thought you'd only called in for a short time. Remember, they may discover your absence at home . . .'

'What then?'

'They'll search for you, and find you . . .'

'What then?'

'Elena Nikolayevna . . . you see, he can't protect you now.'

She looked down as if in thought, put her handkerchief to her lips and broke into convulsive, overwhelming sobs . . . She threw herself face down on to the sofa, trying to stifle them, but her whole body heaved and throbbed like the body of a captured bird.

'Elena Nikolayevna . . . for God's sake!' Bersyenev repeated, standing over her.

'What is it?' Insarov's voice broke in suddenly.

Elena sat upright and Bersyenev stood motionless. Then he went up to the bed; as before, Insarov's head lay lifelessly on the pillow and his eyes were closed.

'Is he wandering?' Elena whispered.

'It seems so,' Bersyenev answered, 'but it doesn't mean anything – that always happens too, especially if . . .'

'When was he taken ill?' Elena interrupted.

'Two days ago . . . I've been here since yesterday. You must rely on me, Elena Nikolayevna. I shan't leave him; everything possible will be done. If necessary we shall take other advice.'

'He'll die without me!' she cried, wringing her hands.

'I promise to let you know how it goes on, I'll let you know every day, and if it becomes really critical . . .'

'Swear that you'll send for me at once – whenever it is, day or night – send a note direct to me . . . nothing matters now. Do you hear? Do you promise?'

'Before God I promise.'

'Swear it.'

'I swear it.'

Suddenly she grasped his hand, and before he could withdraw it, she pressed it to her lips.

'Elena Nikolayevna, what are you doing?' he stammered.

'No . . . no . . . you mustn't,' Insarov said indistinctly, with a deep sigh.

Elena went up to the screen, gripping her handkerchief between her teeth and gazed long and intently at the sick man. She wept silently and the tears ran down her cheeks.

'Elena Nikolayevna,' Bersyenev said, 'he may regain consciousness and recognize you; God knows whether that would be a good thing. Besides, I'm expecting the doctor at any moment.'

Elena picked up her hat from the sofa, put it on and stood still. Her eyes roamed sadly round the room as if she were remembering . . .

'I can't go,' she whispered at last.

Bersyenev pressed her hand.

'You must be strong,' he said, 'and calm. You're leaving him in my care; I shall call in tonight to see you, without fail.'

She glanced at him and said: 'Oh, my good friend!' Then she rushed away, sobbing.

He leaned against the door. Grief and bitterness oppressed him, though his feelings were not without a queer sense of consolation. 'My good friend!' he thought, and shrugged his shoulders.

'Who's here?' he heard Insarov say. He went up to the bed.

'I am here, Dmitri Nikanorovich. What is it? How are you feeling?'

'Are you alone?'

'Yes.'

'Where is she?'

'She? Who?' Bersyenev said, almost afraid.

Insarov was silent for a moment.

'Mignonette,' he murmured, and his eyes closed again.

XXVI

FOR eight full days Insarov lay between life and death. The doctor came continually; young man as he was, he was interested in a difficult case. Shubin heard of Insarov's serious condition, and visited him; compatriots of his, Bulgarians, also made an appearance; among them Bersyenev recognized the two strange individuals whose unexpected visit at the cottage had so astonished him. All expressed deep concern, and several offered to take Bersyenev's place at the bedside; but he, remembering his promise to Elena, would not agree. He saw her every day; surreptitiously, either verbally, or by means of a note, he gave her full details of how the malady was progressing. With what deep anxiety she awaited him, how intently she listened to him and questioned him! She was continually fretting to go to Insarov herself, but Bersyenev implored her not to; Insarov was seldom alone. The first day she had heard of his illness, she had almost fallen ill herself. As soon as she returned home, she had locked herself in her room; but they had sent for her to dinner and she had entered the room looking so ill that Anna Vassilyevna was alarmed and wanted to send her to bed at once. However, Elena succeeded in overcoming her feelings. 'If he dies,' she kept saying, 'I shall go too.' This thought comforted her and gave her strength to appear unconcerned. But as it happened no one worried her unduly: Anna Vassilyevna was troubled with her gumboils; Shubin was in a frenzy of work; Zoya had fallen into a fit of melancholy and had decided to read *Werther*. Nikolai Artyomevich was very displeased at the frequent visits of Bersyenev the 'scholar', more particularly as his 'project' with regard to Kurnatovski was going slowly – the matter-of-fact chief secretary seemed uncertain and was biding his time. Elena did not even thank Bersyenev: there are some kindnesses for which it is too painful and embarrassing to offer thanks. Only once, on his fourth visit, after Insarov had passed a very bad night and the doctor had hinted at a consultation, did she remind him of his promise. 'Very well, then,' he said, 'let us go.' She got up and was going to put on her cape. 'No,' he said, 'wait till tomorrow.' By the evening Insarov was a little better.

For eight days the agony went on. Elena appeared calm, but could eat nothing, and did not sleep at nights. There was a dull ache in her limbs, a sort of hot, dry sensation in her head. 'Our young mistress is melting away like a candle,' her maid would say.

At last, on the ninth day, the crisis came. Elena was sitting in the drawing-room beside Anna Vassilyevna, reading the *Moscow Journal* to her, and hardly knowing what she did. Then Bersyenev entered. Elena glanced at him with that quick, shy, penetrating anxious glance with which she met him every time he came – and at once she guessed that he had brought good news. He nodded to her, smiling, and she rose in her seat to greet him.

'He's conscious again and out of danger; in a week he will be quite well,' he whispered to her.

Elena put out her hand, as if averting a blow, and said nothing; only her lips trembled and her face flushed crimson. Bersyenev began to talk to Anna Vassilyevna, and Elena went to her room, where she fell on her knees and prayed and thanked God . . . gentle, carefree tears came to her eyes. Suddenly she felt utterly exhausted. She laid her head on the pillow, whispered: 'Poor Andrei Petrovich' . . . and there and then fell asleep, with her eyelashes and cheeks still wet. It was long since she had slept or wept.

XXVII

BERSYENEV'S news turned out to be only partly true: the danger was past, but Insarov recovered his strength only slowly, and the doctor spoke of a profound shock to his whole constitution. Nevertheless, the sick man got up and began to walk about the room. Bersyenev had returned to his rooms but each day he called in to see his friend, who was still very weak, and each day, as before, he reported to Elena on the state of the patient's health. Insarov did not dare to write to her, and referred to her only indirectly in conversation with Bersyenev; but Bersyenev, with assumed indifference, told him of his visits to the Stahovs, and tried at the same time to convey that Elena had been deeply distressed, though she was now at ease again. Elena did not write either; she had another project in mind.

One day, Bersyenev, looking very cheerful, told her that the doctor had allowed Insarov to eat a cutlet and that he would probably be going out shortly; as soon as he had spoken Elena looked down thoughtfully.

'Can you guess what I want to say to you?' she asked.

Bersyenev felt embarrassed; he understood her.

'I expect you want to tell me that you'd like to see him,' he answered, looking away from her.

Elena blushed and murmured half-audibly: 'Yes.'

'Well, why not? I should think you can do that easily enough,' he said, conscious at the same time of a sickening sensation in his heart.

'You mean, because I've been there already?' Elena said.

'But you see I'm afraid ... you say he's seldom alone now.'

'That's no problem,' Bersyenev replied, still looking away from her. 'I can't warn him personally, of course, but you can give me a note. No one can stop your writing to him as to a good friend for whom you feel concern. There's nothing reprehensible in that. Make a . . . I mean, write and tell him when you're coming.'

'It's so difficult,' Elena whispered.

'Give me a note and I'll take it to him.'

'That's not necessary, but I did want to ask you something – don't be cross with me, Andrei Petrovich – please don't go to him tomorrow.'

Bersyenev bit his lip.

'Oh! I understand, perfectly, perfectly,' he said, and after a word or two more, he quickly made his departure.

'All the better, all the better,' he thought, as he hurried home. 'I didn't find out anything new to encourage me, but perhaps it's just as well. What's the pleasure in hanging around someone else's back garden? I don't regret anything, I simply did what my conscience told me to do – but now it's over. Let them be! My father was right when he said: "We're not Sybarites, my boy, we're not aristocrats, the spoilt children of destiny, we're not even martyrs – no, we're just workers, workers, workers. Put on your leather apron, worker, and get to your bench in your dark workshop! Leave the sunshine to other people. There's pride and happiness even in our obscure existence."'

The next morning the postman brought Insarov a tiny note from Elena: 'Expect me,' she wrote, 'and tell them to keep everyone away. A.P. will not be coming.'

XXVIII

As soon as Insarov had read Elena's note he set about tidying his room; he asked the landlady to clear away the medicine bottles, took off his dressing-gown and put on his jacket. His heart was thumping and he felt giddy with joy and weakness. His legs gave way under him: he sat down on the sofa and looked at his watch. 'A quarter to twelve,' he said to himself, 'she can't possibly be here before twelve. I must think of something else for a quarter of an hour, otherwise I shan't survive it. She can't possibly be here before twelve o'clock. . . .'

Suddenly the door was flung open and Elena entered. Pale and fresh in a light silk frock, looking so young and happy, she fell on his breast with a faint cry of joy.

'You are alive,' she repeated again and again, 'you are mine!' She took his head in her arms and caressed it; he felt faint and breathless at the touch of her hands, at her closeness to him, at his own happiness.

She sat down and nestled up to him and gazed at him with the laughing, tender, caressing look which shines only in the eyes of a woman in love.

Suddenly her face clouded.

'How thin you've got, my poor Dmitri,' she said, passing her hand over his cheek, 'how your beard has grown!'

'And you've grown thin too, my poor Elena,' he replied, catching her fingers with a kiss.

She shook her curls gaily.

'That's nothing – you just see how we're going to get

better! The storm blew up just as it did that day we met in the shrine, it came and it passed away. Now we're going to live!'

He only smiled in answer.

'Oh, what a time it's been, Dmitri, what a cruel time! How can people bear to live on after those they love have gone? Honestly, I always knew in advance what Andrei Petrovich was going to tell me; my life just hung on yours. Welcome back to life, Dmitri!'

He did not know what to say to her. He felt he wanted to fall at her feet.

'Something else I noticed,' she went on, brushing back his hair. 'I noticed so many things all that time when I had nothing to do – you know, when a person is very, very unhappy, he examines everything that's going on around him with an absurd, minute attention. Honestly, sometimes I'd stare and stare at a fly, though there was a chill terror in my heart. But that's all over, it is all over, isn't it? Everything's bright ahead of us, isn't it?'

'For me, you are ahead,' he answered, 'it's bright for me.'

'And for me too! But do you remember the last time I was here – no, not the last time,' she said, with an involuntary shudder – 'but when we were talking together, and I began to talk about death – I don't know why; I little suspected that death was lurking near us then. But you are better now, aren't you?'

'I'm much better, almost quite well.'

'You're well – you didn't die. Oh, how happy I am!'

They were silent for a while.

'Elena,' he said.

'What is it, my darling?'

'Tell me, has it ever occurred to you that this illness was sent as a punishment to us?'

Elena glanced at him gravely.

'The idea did occur to me, Dmitri. But then I thought, what should I be punished for? How have I failed in my duty, how have I offended? Maybe my conscience is different from other people's, but anyway it was at rest; or can it be that I'm to blame on your account: shall I be hindering you, shall I stop you? . . .'

'You won't stop me, Elena, we shall go together.'

'Yes, Dmitri, we shall go together, I shall go where you go . . . That's my duty. I love you . . . I don't know any other duty.'

'Oh, Elena!' Insarov said, 'somehow every word you say puts me in everlasting chains.'

'Why talk of chains?' she retorted, 'we are both free human beings. Yes,' she went on, looking thoughtfully at the floor and still smoothing his hair with her hand, 'so much I've lived through these last days, so much that I never had an idea of before! If anyone had told me before that I – a well-brought-up young lady – would be going out alone under all sorts of false pretexts, and had told me where I'd be going to, to see a young man in his lodgings – how indignant I should have been! And yet all that has come to pass, and I don't feel indignant at all. Yes, it's true,' she added, turning to Insarov.

He looked at her with such adoration that she gently dropped her hand from his hair and covered his eyes.

'Dmitri,' she began again, 'you don't know, do you, that I saw you there on that awful bed . . . I saw you in death's clutches, unconscious –'

'You saw me?'

'Yes.'

He was silent for a moment.

'Was Bersyenev here too?'

She nodded her head. He leaned towards her.

'Oh, Elena!' he whispered. 'I don't dare to look at you.'

'Why? Andrei Petrovich is so kind! I didn't feel ashamed in front of him. And what have I to be ashamed of? I'm ready to tell the whole world that I belong to you ... But Andrei Petrovich I trust as if he were a brother.'

'He saved my life!' Insarov cried. 'He's the kindest and most generous of men.'

'Yes ... And did you know that I owe everything to him. Did you know it was he who first told me that you loved me? And if I could tell you everything ... yes, he is the most generous of men.'

Insarov looked at her intently.

'He's in love with you, isn't he?'

She looked down.

'He did love me,' she said quietly.

Insarov squeezed her hand.

'Oh, you Russians,' he said, 'what hearts of gold you have! There's Bersyenev, how he looked after me, and sat up at nights! And you, too, my angel – with never a reproach, never a sign of hesitation ... and all this for me ...'

'Yes, yes, all for you – because we love you. Oh, Dmitri, how strange it is! I think I've spoken to you about this before, but never mind, I shall like telling you again, and you'll like to hear it again – when I first saw you –'

'Why are there tears in your eyes?' Insarov interrupted.

'Tears in my eyes?' She wiped them away with her handkerchief. 'You foolish man, you still don't know that you can weep for happiness! But what I wanted to say was this: when I saw you the first time I didn't think you at all remarkable, really I didn't. I liked Shubin much more at first, though I never loved him – and as for Andrei Petrovich, oh yes, there was a moment when I did ask myself, is this indeed the man? But with you, there was nothing; yet afterwards – afterwards – how you seized hold of my heart with both your hands.'

'Don't, don't –' Insarov said. He tried to stand up, but at once fell back on the sofa.

'What's the matter?' she asked anxiously.

'Nothing . . . I'm still not very strong – happiness like this is still too much for my strength.'

'Then you must just sit quietly. You must keep quite still and not get excited,' she said, shaking her finger at him. 'And why did you take off your dressing-gown? It's too soon to be showing off yet. Just sit here and I'll tell you stories. You must listen and not say anything. It's harmful to talk a lot when you've been ill.'

She began to talk to him about Shubin and Kurnatovski, and what she had done during the last two weeks; she told him that war, according to the papers, was inevitable, and that consequently, as soon as he was quite better, they would have to find means of getting away without a moment's delay . . . So she talked to him, sitting at his side, leaning her arm on his shoulder . . .

He listened to her, now flushing, now turning pale; several times he tried to stop her – then suddenly he sat up.

'Elena,' he said, in a queer, brusque tone of voice, 'leave me, you must go away.'

'What do you mean?' she said with astonishment. 'Aren't you feeling well?' she added quickly.

'No – I'm all right, but please leave me.'

'I don't understand you. Are you sending me away? . . . What are you doing?' she asked suddenly; he had leaned down almost to the floor and was kissing her feet. 'Don't do that, Dmitri . . . Dmitri . . .'

He sat up.

'Then you must leave me! You see, Elena, when I fell ill I didn't lose consciousness at first, and I knew then that I was on the edge of the abyss; even when I was feverish and delirious I realized it, I had a dim feeling that death was near, and I said good-bye to life and to you and to everything, and I lost all hope . . . And now suddenly this rebirth, this light after darkness, and you – you next to me, with me here – your voice, your breathing – it's too much for me to stand! I feel how passionately I love you, I hear you say you belong to me, and I can't answer for myself . . . You must go!'

'Dmitri,' she whispered, and hid her face on his shoulder. Only now she understood him.

'Elena,' he went on, 'I love you, you know that, and I'd willingly give my life for you . . . but why do you come to me now, when I'm weak and not in control of myself – when my blood is on fire – you say you belong to me, you love me . . .'

'Dmitri,' she repeated; she flushed and pressed still closer to him.

'Elena, have pity on me, you must go, I feel I might die . . . I can't bear these feelings – all my being is longing for you . . . to think that death almost parted us . . . and now you're here in my arms . . . Elena.'

She trembled.

'Then take me,' she whispered, so that he hardly heard . . .

XXIX

NIKOLAI ARTYOMEVICH was walking up and down his
study with a frown on his face; Shubin was sitting by the
window with his knees crossed, calmly smoking a cigar.

'I wish you'd stop marching from one end of the room
to the other,' he said, knocking the ash from his cigar. 'I
keep expecting you to say something, and this twisting
my head backwards and forwards to follow you makes my
neck ache. Besides, there's something so tense and melo-
dramatic in the way you walk.'

'All you care about is being facetious,' Nikolai Artyomevich answered. 'You make no effort to understand what
I feel, you will not realize that I've got used to this woman,
that I'm fond of her in fact, so that it's naturally a torment
for me when she's away ... It's October already, winter
is almost upon us. What can she be doing in Reval?'

'Maybe she's knitting stockings – for herself, not for
you.'

'You may laugh, you may laugh – but I assure you I
don't know another woman like her. So honest, so disinterested . . .'

'Did she claim the money on the promissory note?'
Shubin asked.

'So disinterested,' Nikolai Artyomevich repeated, raising
his voice, 'it's really astonishing. They tell me there are
millions of other women, but I say show me them, show
me these millions of women, I say: *ces femmes – qu'on me les
montre!* And she doesn't write – that's what's killing me.'

'You're as eloquent as Pythagoras,' Shubin remarked. 'Do you know what I'd advise you to do?'

'What?'

'When Avgustina Christianovna returns ... d'you see what I mean?'

'Well, what about it?'

'When you see her ... d'you follow my train of thought?'

'Yes, yes.'

'Try giving her a good thrashing. See what that will do.'

Nikolai Artyomevich turned away in indignation.

'I really thought you were going to give me some worthwhile advice – but what can one expect from an artist, a man without principles ...'

'Without principles ... yet I hear that your favourite, Mr Kurnatovski, won a hundred roubles off you yesterday in spite of all his principles. That was tactless, you'll agree.'

'What about it? We were playing for money. Of course, I would have expected ... But he's so little appreciated in this house –'

'That he thinks to himself: "To hell with it! Whether he's to become my father-in-law is still in the lap of the Gods, but a hundred roubles is well worth while to a fellow who doesn't take bribes!"'

'Father-in-law? – father-in-law be damned! *Vous revez, mon cher*. Of course, any other young girl would be delighted at having such a suitor. You can judge for yourself: energetic, intelligent – made his own way in the world – worked through two provinces –'

'In the Province of —— he had the governor by the nose,' Shubin observed.

'Very possibly: I dare say that was needful. A practical man, a business man –'

'A good card-player,' Shubin put in again.

'All right, he plays cards well, too. But as for Elena Nikolayevna – can anyone understand her? I'd like to meet the man who'd undertake to find out what she wanted. First she's cheerful, then she's pining away – she suddenly gets so thin that you can hardly bear to look at her, and then suddenly gets better again; and all this without any apparent cause.'

An ill-favoured footman came in bearing a cup of coffee, a cream-jug and some rusks on a tray.

'The father likes the young man,' Nikolai Artyomevich continued, brandishing a rusk, 'but what does that matter to the daughter? That sort of thing was well enough in the old patriarchal days, but now we've changed all that: *nous avons changé tout ça*. Now a young lady talks to whom she likes and reads what she likes. She sets off across Moscow without a footman or maid just as they do in Paris – and it's all taken for granted. The other day I asked "Where's Elena Nikolayevna?" – "She's gone out," they tell me – "Where to?" – Nobody knows. Is that right?'

'Do take your coffee and let the man go away,' Shubin said; 'you say yourself you shouldn't – *devant les domestiques*,' he added in an undertone.

The servant looked at Shubin glumly, while Nikolai Artyomevich picked up the cup, poured himself some cream, and took a handful of rusks.

'I wanted to say,' he went on, as soon as the servant had gone, 'that I just don't count for anything in this house – that's all. That's because nowadays everybody judges by appearances: an empty-headed fool is respected provided he behaves self-importantly; whereas another quite possibly has talents which might be of great value to the world, but out of modesty –'

'Do you fancy yourself as a statesman, Nicky?' Shubin asked in a high, piping voice.

'Stop playing the fool,' Nikolai Artyomevich exclaimed angrily, 'you forget yourself. That's just another proof that I don't count for anything in this house, I don't count for anything!'

'Anna Vassilyevna persecutes you so . . . poor little man,' said Shubin, stretching. 'Oh, Nikolai Artyomevich, really we ought to be ashamed of ourselves. You'd be better occupied finding a present for Anna Vassilyevna – it will be her birthday in a day or two, and you know how she values the least sign of attention on your part.'

'Yes, yes,' Nikolai Artyomevich answered quickly, 'I'm very grateful to you for reminding me. Of course, of course, I must certainly . . . As a matter of fact, I've got a small thing here: a clasp, I got it the other day at Rosenstrauch's. Only I really don't know whether it will suit her.'

'You bought it for the lady in Reval, didn't you?'

'As a matter of fact – well, yes – I was thinking –'

'In that case it's sure to suit her.'

Shubin got up from the chair.

'Where shall we go tonight, Pavel Yakovlevich, eh?' Nikolai Artyomevich asked him genially, looking him in the eyes.

'Aren't you going to the club?'

'I mean after the club – afterwards.'

Shubin stretched again.

'No, Nikolai Artyomevich, I've got to work tomorrow. Another time.' And he went out.

Nikolai Artyomevich frowned and crossed the room two or three times; then he took from the bureau the velvet-lined box containing the clasp, which he gazed at intently as he wiped it with his silk handkerchief. He sat down in front of the mirror and, with a grave expression on his face, carefully began to comb his hair, leaning his head now to one side, now to the other, sticking his tongue in his cheek and gazing fixedly at the parting all the while.

Somebody coughed behind him; he looked round and saw the footman who had brought the coffee.

'Nikolai Artyomevich,' the footman said, with a certain solemn dignity, 'you are our master, sir!'

'I know. What of it?'

'Nikolai Artyomevich, forgive me for taking the liberty, sir, only I've been in your service since I was a child, and it's only because of my humble desire to serve you, sir, but I feel I must report –'

'What is it, then?'

The servant stood hesitating.

'You said, sir, you didn't know where Elena Nikola-yevna goes to. I've found out where it is, sir.'

'What's this nonsense, you blockhead?'

'As you please, sir – but three days ago I saw her going into a certain house.'

'What? Where? What house?'

'In the — Street, near the Povarskaya, not far from here. I asked the porter what lodgers they had there.'

Nikolai Artyomevich stamped his foot.

'Silence, scoundrel! My daughter, in her goodness of heart, goes visiting the poor, and you . . . Get out, you fool!'

The terrified servant rushed to the door.

'Stop!' cried Nikolai Artyomevich. 'What did the porter say?'

'Nothing – nothing, sir. He said a – a student.'

'Silence, wretch! . . . Listen, if you ever let out a word about this to anyone, even in your sleep –'

'But, please, sir . . .'

'Silence! If you utter a single word – if anyone tells me – if I get to hear of it – I'll catch you if you're hiding at the bottom of the sea! D'you hear? Clear out!'

The servant vanished.

'Oh, my God, my God! What does it all mean?' Nikolai Artyomevich thought when he was left alone. 'What's the idiot been telling me? Anyway, I must find out what house it is, who lives there – I'll have to go round myself. So that's what it's come to . . . a servant, *un laquais* . . . *quelle humiliation*!'

And loudly repeating '*un laquais*', he locked up the clasp in the bureau and went to see Anna Vassilyevna. He found her in bed with her face bandaged up; but the sight of her suffering only irritated him, and he very soon reduced her to tears.

XXX

MEANWHILE the storm which had been gathering in the Balkans broke at last. Turkey declared war on Russia; the date appointed for the evacuation of the Principalities was past, the day of the Sinope 'massacre' was near at hand. The last letters which Insarov had received summoned him urgently home. His health was still not mended; he was coughing, he felt weak, and was subject to slight attacks of fever; nevertheless he hardly ever stayed at home. His mind was aflame, and he no longer gave a thought to his illness. He went about Moscow continuously, meeting all sorts of people secretly; he would write all night and disappear for whole days. He told his landlord he would be going away soon, and made him a gift of his simple furniture. On her part Elena also made preparations for their departure. One wet evening, as she was sitting in her room, hemming handkerchiefs and listening with irresistible depression to the howling of the wind, her maid came in and told her that her father was in her mother's bedroom and wanted to see her there . . . 'Your Mama is crying,' she whispered as Elena went out, 'and your Papa is in a temper.'

Elena shrugged her shoulders and went into the bedroom. She found her good-natured mother reclining in a lean-back chair and sniffing eau-de-cologne from her handkerchief: her father was standing by the fireplace. With his jacket buttoned up, and his stiff cravat worn high on his well-starched collar, his demeanour was somehow reminiscent of a parliamentary orator. With a dramatic movement of his arm he pointed to a chair; and when his daughter failed to understand his gesture, and looked at him questioningly, he said, speaking with dignity, but without turning towards her: 'Kindly be seated.'

Elena sat down. Her mother blew her nose tearfully. Nikolai Artyomevich put his right hand under his jacket.

'I sent for you, Elena Nikolayevna,' he began, after a long pause, 'in order that we may explain ourselves to one another – or rather I should say, in order to demand an explanation from you. I am displeased with you – no, that is too mild an expression; I am grieved and outraged at your behaviour – I and your mother, too . . . your mother, whom you see sitting here.'

Nikolai Artyomevich spoke in a deep bass tone of voice. Elena looked at him in silence, then looked at her mother and turned pale.

'There was a time,' Nikolai Artyomevich began again, 'when daughters did not permit themselves to disdain their parents, when rebellious children trembled at parental authority; that time is past, unfortunately – at least, many people think it is; but believe me, there still exist laws which do not permit, which do not permit . . . in short, there exist laws. Pray take notice of that: there exist laws!'

'But, Papa!' Elena was beginning.

'Pray do not interrupt me. Let us consider the past. Anna Vassilyevna and I have done our duty. Anna Vassilyevna and I have spared nothing for your education, neither expense nor pains. What profit you have derived from our expense and pains is another matter; but I had the right to expect – Anna Vassilyevna and I had the right to expect

191

– that you would at least strictly observe those principles of morality which we have . . . *que nous vous avons inculqués* . . . which we have impressed upon you as our only daughter. We had the right to expect that none of these modern "ideas" would be allowed to affect this, so to speak, sacred obligation. Yet what do we find? I do not refer now to that frivolity which is natural to your age and sex – but who would have expected that you would have so far forgotten yourself . . .'

'Papa,' Elena put in, 'I know what you're going to say . . .'

'No, you don't know what I'm going to say,' cried Nikolai Artyomevich in high falsetto, suddenly abandoning his parliamentary manner, his fluent pomposity and his booming tone – 'you don't know, you insolent girl . . .'

'For heaven's sake, Nikolai,' murmured Anna Vassilyevna, 'you'll be the death of me.'

'Don't say that to me – don't you say I'll be the death of you, Anna Vassilyevna! You can't conceive what I'm going to tell you now – prepare for the worst, I'm warning you!'

Anna Vassilyevna almost went into a faint.

'No,' Nikolai Artyomevich continued, turning to Elena, 'you don't know what I'm going to say!'

'I've acted wrongly towards you,' she began.

'Ah-ha! At last!'

'I've acted wrongly towards you,' Elena went on, 'because I did not confess to you long ago –'

'And do you realize,' Nikolai Artyomevich interrupted, 'that I can destroy you with one word?'

Elena looked up at him.

'Yes, madam, just one word – it's no good staring!' He folded his arms. 'May I ask if you know a certain house in the — Street, near the Povarskaya? Have you visited that house?' He stamped his foot. 'Answer me, you worthless girl, don't try to hide it! The servants saw you, madam, the servants saw you, *de vils laquais*, as you went in – to your –'

Elena flushed crimson and her eyes flashed.

'There's no need for me to hide anything,' she said; 'yes, I did go to the house.'

'Excellent! D'you hear that, Anna Vassilyevna? And I daresay you know who lives there?'

'Yes, I know: my husband.'

Nikolai Artyomevich's eyes bulged.

'Your . . .'

'My husband,' Elena repeated. 'I am married to Dmitri Nikanorovich Insarov.'

'You . . . married,' whispered Anna Vassilyevna, hardly managing to utter the words.

'Yes, Mamma, forgive me. A fortnight ago we were secretly married.'

Anna Vassilyevna slumped into the chair; Nikolai Artyomevich retreated two paces.

'Married! To that tramp, that Montenegrin! The daughter of Nikolai Stahov, a member of our ancient, noble family, goes and gets married to a mere plebeian, a tramp. Without her parents' blessing, too! And you imagine I'm going to leave it at that? That I won't lodge a complaint? D'you think I'll let your . . . that you . . . that . . . I'll put you in a nunnery – and as for him, I'll send him to hard labour with the convicts. Anna Vassilyevna, kindly tell her you disinherit her, at once!'

'Nikolai Artyomevich, for heaven's sake,' groaned Anna Vassilyevna.

'When did this happen, how? Who married you,

where? How? My God, what will our friends say, what will all the world say now? You shameless hypocrite, to think you could stay here under your parents' roof after doing such a thing! Didn't you fear ... the wrath of God?'

'Papa,' Elena said – she was trembling all over, but her voice was firm – 'you can do what you like with me, but you're not justified in accusing me of shamelessness and hypocrisy. I didn't want to distress you any sooner – but I would have had to tell you everything in a day or two, because I'm leaving here next week with my husband.'

'You're leaving? ...Where are you going to?'

'To his own country, to Bulgaria.'

'To the Turks!' Anna Vassilyevna cried, and fainted.

Elena rushed towards her mother.

'Get away!' Nikolai Artyomevich cried, grasping his daughter by the arm. 'Get away, you worthless girl!'

But just then the door opened and Shubin's head appeared; his face was pale and his eyes flashing.

'Nikolai Artyomevich!' he cried at the top of his voice, 'Avgustina Christianovna is here and wants to see you!'

Nikolai Artyomevich turned on him furiously and shook his fist at him; he stood still for a moment and then quickly left the room.

Elena fell at her mother's feet and embraced her knees.

* * *

Uvar Ivanovich lay on his bed. His collarless shirt, held together round his fat neck by a massive stud, fell apart in loose folds over his almost womanly bosom, and revealed a large cyprus-wood cross and a small bag of sacred relics which he wore as amulets. A light counterpane covered his vast limbs. On the bedside table a candle flickered feebly, and by its side stood a mug of kvass. At his feet, sitting gloomily on the bed, was Shubin.

'Yes,' Shubin was saying thoughtfully, 'she's married and she's preparing to go away. Your nephew's been shouting the house down – he shut himself up in the bedroom for the sake of secrecy, but not only the servants, even the coachmen could hear everything he said. And even now he's still raging – he almost came to blows with me, and he keeps threatening her with his paternal vengeance, but it's quite futile, it won't come to anything. Her mother's in despair, but she's much more distressed about her daughter going away than about the marriage.'

Uvar Ivanovich waggled his fingers.

'She's her mother,' he said. 'I mean to say ...'

'Your nephew is threatening to lodge a protest with the archbishop and the governor-general and the minister – but it will all end up with her going away. After all, it's not very pleasant to ruin your own daughter, He's on his high horse now, but he'll have to climb down.'

'They wouldn't have the right to ...' Uvar Ivanovich said, taking a sip from the mug.

'I know, I know ... But what a storm of gossip and criticism there'll be in Moscow. She wasn't afraid of that ... Anyway, she's above all that. She's going away, and think where to – it's horrible just to think of it. So far away, so off-the-map! And what will be waiting for her when she gets there? I can just see her setting off in the night from some inn, in a snow-storm with thirty degrees of frost. She's abandoning her country and her family, but I can understand her. Who's she leaving behind her, who's she been seeing here, anyway? The Kurnatovskis and the Bersyenevs, and people like us – and we're the best of them.

What will she have to regret when she's gone? But there's one bad thing about it all: they say her husband – God, how that word sticks in my throat – they say Insarov's coughing blood; that's bad. I saw him the other day: you might have modelled Brutus from his face there and then . . . Do you know who Brutus was, Uvar Ivanovich?'

'Why should I know? Some man.'

'Precisely: "this was a man". Yes, it's a fine face, but it's sick, very sick . . .'

'It's all the same . . . for fighting with.'

'Quite: it's all the same for fighting with. How perfectly you express yourself today. But it's not all the same for living with – and she will want to have a bit of life with him, you know.'

'Well, that's youth,' Uvar Ivanovich observed.

'Yes, it's youth and glory and courage. It's life and death, struggle, defeat and triumph, love, liberty and fatherland! How fine, how fine! God grant everyone as much! That's not like sitting up to your neck in a bog and taking up an attitude of brave indifference, when in point of fact you don't care anyway. With them, it's a case of keying themselves up to play to the whole world, or perish!'

Shubin's head fell forward on to his chest.

'Yes,' he went on, after a long silence, 'Insarov is worthy of her. And yet what nonsense that is! Nobody's worthy of her. Insarov . . . Insarov . . . What's the point of all this false modesty? Let's admit he's got courage and knows how to stand up for himself – up to now he's not achieved any more than we poor sinners, so are we really such wash-outs? Well, take me, am I such a wash-out, Uvar Ivanovich? Has God been altogether unkind to me? Hasn't he given me any ability or talent? Who knows, maybe Pavel Shubin will be a famous name in time to come. Look at that half-penny of yours on the table there: perhaps a hundred years hence that bit of copper will go towards a statue erected in honour of Pavel Shubin by a grateful posterity!'

Uvar Ivanovich leaned on his elbow and stared at the excited artist.

'That's a long time yet,' he said at last, waggling his fingers. 'We were talking about the others, but you . . . I mean . . . you start talking about yourself.'

'O great philosopher of the Russian soil!' Shubin exclaimed. 'Every word you utter is pure gold: it shouldn't be me that they put up a statue for, but you – and I'll take on the job myself! Just as you're lying there, in that very pose – so that you can't say whether there's more power or laziness in it – that's how I'll do it! How justly you struck at my egoism and self-esteem. You're right, you're right: it's no good bragging and talking about oneself. We haven't got anyone among us, no real people, wherever you look. It's all either minnows and mice and little Hamlets feeding on themselves in ignorance and dark obscurity, or braggarts throwing their weight about, wasting time and breath and blowing their own trumpets. Or else there's the other kind, always studying themselves in disgusting detail, feeling their pulses with every sensation that they experience and then reporting to themselves: "That's how I feel, and that's what I think." What a useful, sensible sort of occupation. No, if we'd had some proper people among us, that girl, that sensitive spirit, wouldn't have left us, she wouldn't have slipped out of our hands like a fish into the water. Why is it, Uvar Ivanovich? When is our time coming? When are we going to produce some real people?'

'Wait a bit,' Uvar Ivanovich replied, 'they'll come.'

'They'll come? The good earth speaks, the spirit of the black soil says: "They'll come"? You look out – I'll make a note of what you say! But why are you blowing out the candle?'

'I want to go to sleep. Good night.'

XXXI

SHUBIN had told the truth: the unexpected news of Elena's marriage almost killed Anna Vassilyevna, and she took to her bed. Nikolai Artyomevich insisted that she should not allow her daughter into her presence; he seemed to be enjoying the chance of showing himself master of the house in the fullest sense, the real head of the family. He blustered and raged incessantly at the servants, every now and then telling them: 'I'll show you who I am – you'll see soon enough – you just wait.' While he was at home Anna Vassilyevna did not see Elena, and contented herself with Zoya's company; the young German looked after her very attentively as she thought to herself: 'Fancy preferring Insarov to *him*.' But as soon as Nikolai Artyomevich went out – and this happened fairly frequently, as Avgustina Christianovna had really returned – Elena would go into the bedroom and her mother would gaze at her long and silently, with tears in her eyes. This silent reproach affected Elena more deeply than anything: it was not repentance that she felt then, but a sense of infinite pity which was akin to repentance.

'Mama darling,' she repeated, kissing her hands, 'what could I do? I'm not to blame – I fell in love with him, I couldn't act in any other way. You should blame Fate; it was Fate that brought me together with a man that father didn't like, a man who would take me away from you.'

'Oh, don't remind me of that,' Anna Vassilyevna

interrupted her. 'When I think where you mean to go to, my heart seems to break into pieces.'

'Mama dear,' Elena answered, 'you must comfort yourself with the thought that it might have been even worse: I might have died . . .'

'But even as it is I'm not hoping ever to see you again. Either you'll die out there in some tent' – she pictured Bulgaria as a sort of Siberian tundra – 'or else I shan't get over the separation . . .'

'Don't say that, Mama dear, we shall meet again, please God. And there are towns in Bulgaria just as there are here.'

'Towns? There's a war going on there now: wherever you go there now, I expect they'll be firing off their cannons . . . Do you intend leaving soon?'

'Yes . . . if only Papa . . . you know he wants to complain, and he's threatening to divorce us.'

Anna Vassilyevna raised her eyes to heaven.

'No, Lenochka, he won't complain. I myself would never have agreed to this marriage, I would sooner have died; but what's done can't be undone, I'm not going to let my daughter be disgraced.'

So several days went by: then at last Anna Vassilyevna plucked up her courage, and one evening shut herself up in her bedroom along with her husband. Everyone in the house fell silent and listened intently. At first nothing was audible, then came the drone of Nikolai Artyomevich's voice; an argument started, there were cries, there even seemed to be groans. Shubin, who was with Zoya and the maids, was preparing once more to go to the rescue, when the noise in the bedroom began gradually to subside, turned into quiet conversation, then disappeared. Only occasionally there was a faint sob, and then that also ceased. They heard the jingle of keys and the squeak of a bureau being opened . . . The door opened and Nikolai Artyomevich appeared; looking severely at everyone he met, he set off for the club. Anna Vassilyevna sent for her daughter. Crying bitterly she embraced her warmly, saying:

'Everything's settled, he won't make any trouble . . . and there's nothing to prevent you going away now . . . and leaving us.'

'Will you let Dmitri come and thank you?' Elena asked her mother, as soon as Anna Vassilyevna was a little calmer.

'Wait, my darling, just now I can't bring myself to see the man who has parted us . . . we'll manage it before you go away.'

'Before we go away,' Elena repeated sadly.

Nikolai Artyomevich had agreed not to 'make trouble', but Anna Vassilyevna did not tell her daughter what price he had put on his agreement. She did not tell her that she had promised to pay all his debts, and that she had handed over a thousand roubles to him there and then. In addition he had told Anna Vassilyevna forcibly that he wouldn't see Insarov, whom he persisted in describing as a Montenegrin. Yet when he arrived at the club he began, quite gratuitously, to discuss his daughter's marriage with his partner at cards, a retired General of the Engineers. 'Did you hear about my daughter?' he said, with an assumed air of indifference; 'her learning went to her head to such an extent that she's gone and got married to some student.' The general looked at him through his spectacles, growled 'Huh', and asked him what card he was playing.

XXXII

THE day of the departure drew near. November was almost over; soon it would no longer be practicable to go. Insarov had long completed his preparations, and was eager to escape from Moscow as soon as possible. The doctor, too, urged him to get away quickly: 'You need a warm climate,' he said, 'you'll not mend here.' Elena, also, was filled with impatience: she was alarmed at Insarov's pallor, his loss of weight . . . often she looked at his altered features with an involuntary shudder. Her situation at home was becoming intolerable. Her mother lamented over her as if she were already dead, while her father's attitude was one of cold contempt; he also was secretly tormented at the approaching separation, but he considered it his duty, the duty of an outraged parent, to hide his feelings and his weakness. At last Anna Vassilyevna said she would like to see Insarov. They brought him to her surreptitiously, by a back entrance. When he entered the room she was unable to speak to him for a long time, she could not even bring herself to look at him; he sat down by her arm-chair, and waited in quiet deference for her to say the first word. Elena sat with them, holding her mother's hand. At last Anna Vassilyevna looked up and said: 'God will be your judge, Dmitri Nikanorovich,' then stopped; the reproach died on her lips.

'But you are ill!' she cried. 'Elena, your husband is ill!'

'I have been unwell, Anna Vassilyevna,' Insarov replied,

'and I am still not quite better. But I hope that the air at home will finally restore my health.'

'Yes ... Bulgaria!' Anna Vassilyevna murmured, but she thought: 'My God, a Bulgarian, a dying man, hollow-voiced, with eyes like saucers, yellow as parchment, a bag of bones in a jacket that seems to belong to someone else ... and she's his wife, she loves him – oh, this must be some bad dream!' But she recollected herself at once. 'Dmitri Nikanorovich,' she said, 'is it essential ... is it essential that you go?'

'Yes, essential, Anna Vassilyevna.'

Anna Vassilyevna looked at him.

'Oh, Dmitri Nikanorovich, may you never have to suffer what I am going through now! ... You'll promise me to take care of her and to love her? You'll never need to suffer want while I am alive ...'

Tears drowned her words. She opened her arms and embraced Elena and Insarov together.

* * *

At last the fateful day arrived. It had been decided that Elena should bid farewell to her parents at home, but that the journey should start from Insarov's lodging; they were to leave at twelve o'clock. A quarter of an hour before the appointed time, Bersyenev arrived. He had expected to find Insarov's compatriots there, as he assumed they would want to see him off; but they had all gone on ahead of him. Even the two mysterious individuals with whom the reader is already acquainted – and who, incidentally, had acted as witnesses at the wedding – had also gone. The tailor greeted the 'kind gentleman' with a bow; he had been drinking heavily, probably out of grief, but possibly also out of joy at getting hold of the furniture, and his wife soon took him away. The room had been thoroughly tidied up; the trunk, tied up with cord, stood on the floor. Bersyenev was pensive; a host of memories flooded into his mind.

Twelve o'clock was long past, the coachman had already brought the sleigh to the door, but still no one came. At last hurried footsteps were heard on the staircase, and Elena, escorted by Insarov and Shubin, entered the room. Elena's eyes were red; the parting had been very painful, and she had left her mother in a swoon . . . This was the first time for more than a week that she had seen Bersyenev: recently he had seldom visited the Stahovs and she had not expected to meet him here.

'You!' she cried, running to embrace him. 'Thank you!' Then Insarov embraced him too.

There followed an oppressive silence. What had these three men to say to one another? What feelings were in their hearts? Shubin felt the need for some living sound, some word to break the heavy silence.

'Well, here's our trio again,' he said, 'gathered together for the last time. We must accept our fate, and remember the past with a good will – and with God's help start our new life! "Forward, with God, upon our distant way!"' he began to sing . . . and stopped. Suddenly he felt awkward and ashamed. It seemed wrong to be singing there in the presence of the dead – and at that moment, in that room, the past was dying, that past of which he had been speaking, the past of all who were gathered there. Maybe it was dying in order to give birth to a new life – but nevertheless, it was dying.

'Well, Elena,' Insarov said, turning to his wife, 'that's everything, I think. Everyone's been paid, everything's packed. It only remains to get that trunk downstairs. Landlord!'

The landlord came in with his wife and daughter. Swaying slightly, he listened to Insarov's instructions; then he took the trunk on his shoulders and ran clattering down the stairs.

'And now, according to the Russian custom,' Insarov said, 'we must all sit down.'

They sat down, Bersyenev taking his seat on the old sofa, with Elena by his side. The landlord's wife and daughter crouched on the threshold; all were silent, all were smiling awkwardly, and none could say why they smiled . . . they would all have liked to say some parting words for the occasion, but they all felt that at such a moment it was only possible to talk trivialities, that anything significant or clever, almost that any word of feeling, would somehow seem false and out of place. Insarov was the first to get up.

'Good-bye, little room,' he cried, and crossed himself.

There were kisses all round, good-bye kisses that had sound but no warmth, good wishes for the journey half-expressed, promises to write, those last halting words of farewell . . .

Elena was already seated in the sleigh, her face streaming with tears; Insarov was solicitously covering her legs with a rug; Shubin, Bersyenev, the landlord and his wife and daughter, the porter and some unknown workman in a striped overall, were all standing by the steps – when suddenly a handsome sleigh, drawn by a mettlesome horse, dashed into the yard and halted. Out of it jumped Nikolai Artyomevich, shaking the snow from the collar of his greatcoat.

'Thank God I'm in time,' he cried, and ran to the other sleigh. 'Here, Elena, here's our last blessing for you,' he said, putting his head under the hood, and pulling out of his jacket pocket a small sacred image sewn up in a velvet bag. As he hung it round her neck she began to sob and kiss his hand . . . Meanwhile his coachman had produced from under the box a bottle of champagne and three glasses.

'So now,' Stahov said, and tears kept falling on to the beaver collar of his coat, 'now we must see you . . . we must bid you –' He poured out the champagne; his hand shook, the foam ran over the edge and fell into the snow. He took one glass, gave one to Elena and the other to Insarov, who by now was sitting at her side. 'May God grant you . . .' he began; but he could not finish, and drank the wine . . . Elena and Insarov drank with him. Then Nikolai Artyomevich turned to Shubin and Bersyenev: 'Now you must drink too, gentlemen,' he said; but at that moment the coachman started the horses. Nikolai Artyomevich ran alongside the sleigh. 'Be sure to write to us,' he said unsteadily. Elena put out her head. 'Good-bye Papa,' she said, 'good-bye Andrei Petrovich, Pavel Yakovlevich, good-bye everyone, good-bye Russia!' She leaned back; the coachman cracked his whip and whistled, and the sleigh, grating over the frozen snow, turned out of the gate to the right and vanished.

XXXIII

IT was a bright April day. On the broad lagoon which separates Venice from the Lido – that narrow strip of sand accumulated by the sea – a gondola with pointed prow was gliding slowly, swaying rhythmically with each impulse from the gondolier's long oar. Under the low awning, on soft leather cushions, were sitting Elena and Insarov.

Elena's features had changed little since her departure from Moscow, but her expression was altered; it was sterner and more thoughtful, there was a greater boldness in the eyes. Her whole body had blossomed out, her hair seemed to be growing more thickly and exuberantly around her pale forehead and fresh cheeks. Only the hardly noticeable lines about her mouth – and that only when the smile had left it – showed traces of her secret, never-ceasing anxiety. On the other hand, Insarov's expression was the same as before, but his features were cruelly altered. He had grown thinner, paler, he looked much older, had developed a stoop; he coughed almost continuously with a short, dry cough, and his sunken eyes glittered with a strange brilliance. On the way from Russia he had had to lie up for almost two months in Vienna, and they had come on to Venice only at the end of March; from there he was hoping to make his way by Zara into Serbia and Bulgaria, as the other routes were closed to him. War was already raging on the Danube; France and England had declared war on Russia and all the Slav countries were in turmoil and preparing for insurrection.

The gondola landed at the inner shore of the Lido. Elena and Insarov set off along a narrow sandy path planted with consumptive-looking shrubs (they are put out each spring and die the same year) until they reached the outer, seaward side of the Lido.

They strolled along the shore, with the muddy, deep-blue waters of the Adriatic rolling at their side; foaming and hissing the waves broke in and slid away, leaving on the beach a litter of small shells and scraps of seaweed.

'What a dreary place!' Elena said. 'I'm afraid it may be too cold for you here. But I can guess why you wanted to come.'

'Too cold!' Insarov retorted with a quick, bitter smile. 'I'll make a fine soldier, if I have to be scared of the cold. But as for why I came here – I'll tell you. I look at this sea and I feel as though I'm nearer my country here. It's over there,' he added, stretching out his hand towards the east, 'there where the wind is blowing from.'

'Will this wind bring the ship you're waiting for?' she said. 'Look, there's a white sail, can that be it?'

Insarov looked into the distance, following her out-stretched arm.

'Rèndich promised to arrange things for us within a week,' he said; 'I think we can rely on him . . . Elena,' he added, with sudden animation, 'have you heard what the poor Dalmatian fishermen did with the lumps of lead that they use as weights for their nets? They gave them up for making bullets! They hadn't any money – they only just manage to live by their fishing – yet they gladly gave away their last possessions, and now they're starving. That's a people for you!'

'Look out, there!' a haughty voice shouted behind them. They heard a heavy trampling of hooves, and an Austrian officer, in a short grey tunic and a green peaked cap, galloped past them. They only just managed to get out of his way.

Insarov looked after him morosely.

'He's not to blame,' Elena said. 'You see, they haven't anywhere else to exercise their horses here.'

'No, he's not to blame,' Insarov said, 'but that shout of his and that moustache and peaked cap and everything about him made my blood boil. Let's go back.'

'Yes, we'll go back, Dmitri. Besides, it really is cold here. You didn't take care of yourself after your illness in Moscow, and you paid for it in Vienna. Now you must be more careful.'

Insarov was silent; only that same bitter smile played on his lips.

'I know what we'll do,' Elena went on, 'let's go back by the Grand Canal. You know, we've not seen Venice properly since we've been here. And this evening we're going to the theatre; I've got two tickets for a box. They say they're playing a new opera. Dmitri, just let's give up today to one another, let's forget about politics and the war and everything and only remember that we're alive, and breathing and thinking together, that we belong to one another for ever. Shall we do that?'

'You want to, Elena,' he answered, 'so I can't help wanting to also.'

'I knew it,' Elena said with a smile. 'Now we must go.'

They went back to the gondola and told the boatman to take them, without hurrying, along the Grand Canal.

* * *

No one who has not seen Venice in April knows the full, the indescribable charm of that magical city. The gentleness and softness of spring are to Venice what the bright sun of summer is to majestic Genoa, what the gold and purple of autumn are to that grand old man among cities, Rome. And just as the spring stirs us and fills us with longing, so does the loveliness of Venice; she provokes and tantalizes the innocent heart with a sense of some imminent joy, a joy which is both simple and yet mysterious. Everything about her is light and lucid, yet over everything hangs a drowsy haze of tranquil sensuousness; everything is silent, yet everything is welcoming; everything about her is feminine, even to the very name; not for nothing is she called 'Venice the Beautiful'. The palaces and churches, in their great masses, rise light and miraculous like the harmonious dream creations of some young god; there is something fabulous and enchanting in her grey-green resplendence, in the silky gleam of her silent, rippling canal waters, in the silent movement of the gondolas, in the absence of rude city noises, in the freedom from clatter and turmoil and uproar. 'Venice is dying, Venice is deserted' – so her inhabitants will tell you; but it may be that in the past she lacked such charm as this, the charm of a city fading in the very culmination and flowering of its beauty. No one who has not seen her, knows her: neither Canaletto nor Guardi (not to speak of more recent painters) was able to record the silvery delicacy of her air, her vistas, so near and yet so fugitive, her marvellous harmony of graceful lines and melting colours. To the visitor, soured and broken by life, Venice has nothing to offer; to him she will be bitter as the recollection of early unrealized dreams are bitter. But for him who still has strength and confidence within him, she will be sweet; let him bring his happiness to her and expose it to her enchanted skies, and, however radiant his happiness may be, she will enrich it with her own unfading light.

The gondola in which Insarov and Elena were sitting slipped silently past the Riva degli Schiavoni, the Palace of the Doge and the Piazzetta, and entered the Grand Canal. Along both sides lay the marble palaces; they seemed to float softly by, hardly allowing the eyes time to grasp and take in all their beauty. Elena was profoundly happy; in her azure sky there was but one dark cloud, and that had receded – for Insarov had been much better that day. They were taken as far as the steep arch of the Rialto bridge and then turned back. Elena was afraid of visiting the churches lest Insarov might suffer from the cold; but she remembered the Accademia di Belle Arti, and told the gondolier to take them there. It is a small museum, and they quickly passed through all the galleries. Being neither connoisseurs nor dilettantes, they did not feel compelled to stop and look at every picture; a light-hearted mood had taken possession of them unexpectedly, and everything suddenly appeared highly amusing; it was the kind of hilarious mood that often comes over children. Elena laughed herself to tears over Tintoretto's figure of St Mark, who jumps out of the sky to the rescue of a tortured slave, looking like a frog jumping into the water; and in laughing she scandalized three English visitors to the museum. Insarov, for his part, was greatly delighted at the back and calves of the energetic person in the long green cloak who is seen standing in the foreground of Titian's 'Assumption', stretching out his arms to the Madonna; on the other hand, the Madonna herself, at once strong and beautiful, rising in majestic serenity to the bosom of the Heavenly Father, astonished them both; and they admired, too, a severe sacred painting by the old master Cima da Conegliano. On leaving the Academy they looked round once more at the three Englishmen, with their prominent teeth and pendulous whiskers – and they

began to laugh; they laughed when they caught sight of
their gondolier with his short jacket and trousers; they
laughed still more uproariously when they saw a pedlar-
woman with a knot of grey hair perched on the top of her
head; and finally they looked into each other's eyes and
laughed again; then, as soon as they were settled in the
gondola, how warmly they pressed each other's hands!
They returned to the hotel, hurried to their room, and
ordered dinner to be brought. At dinner their gay humour
did not leave them. They drank each other's health and the
health of their friends in Moscow; they congratulated the
waiter on the delicious fish he had brought them, and then
asked for some live mussels; the waiter shuffled his feet
and shrugged his shoulders, and having left the room
shook his head and muttered with a sigh: 'Poveretti!' (the
poor things). After dinner, they set off for the theatre.

One of Verdi's operas was being performed; it was
Traviata, in truth rather a commonplace piece, but one
which had already successfully made the round of all the
European cities, and which is well known even to us
Russians. The Venice season was over, and none of the
singers achieved more than a dull mediocrity; they just
shouted their parts as loud as they could. Violetta was taken
by a singer without any particular reputation, and judging
by the way the public received her she was not much liked,
though she was not without talent. She was a young girl
with dark eyes and no great beauty; her voice was not quite
steady and had already lost its purity of tone. She was
dressed with an almost painful naïveté in a motley assort-
ment of garments; a red hair-net on her head, a dress of
faded sky-blue satin fitting too tightly round her bosom,
thick suède gloves reaching up to her pointed elbows; and
indeed, how should a girl like this, the daughter of some

peasant from Bergamo, know how the Parisian courtesans dress? She did not even know how to carry herself on the stage; but there was much sincerity and artless simplicity in her playing, and she sang with that peculiarly passionate expression and rhythm which belongs to the Italians alone. Elena and Insarov were sitting alone in the dark box, next to the stage. The gay frame of mind which had taken possession of them in the Accademia di Belle Arti was still with them. When a man in a pea-green tail-coat and a tousled white wig appeared on the scene – he was the father of the unfortunate youth who falls into the clutches of a temptress – opened his mouth slantwise, and, in obvious confusion, gave vent to a dismal bass *tremolo*, both Insarov and Elena almost burst into laughter; but the Violetta made a real impression on them.

'They hardly applaud the poor girl at all,' Elena said, 'yet I prefer her a thousand times to some self-assured, minor celebrity who would just be posing and giving herself airs and striving after effect. It's as if she is really experiencing what she is acting; you can see she doesn't notice the audience.'

Insarov leaned over the box and gazed intently at Violetta.

'Yes,' he said, 'it's the real thing with her; there's a reek of death in the air.'

At that Elena was silent.

The curtain rose on the third act. Elena shuddered at the sight of the bed, the drawn curtains, the medicine bottles, the shaded lamp – it all brought to mind visions of the recent past. 'And what of the present, the future?' The grim question flashed through her mind . . . As if in answer to the assumed cough of the actress on the stage came the hollow sound of Insarov's unfeigned cough at her

213

side. Elena looked at him surreptitiously, and at once her face assumed a calm, serene expression; Insarov read her thoughts, he smiled and began to accompany the singing under his breath.

But he was soon silent again. The young singer's performance was gaining in strength and freedom all the time. She seemed to rid herself of everything unnecessary, everything irrelevant, and – what is the rarest, highest pleasure for any artist – to *find herself*. Suddenly she seemed to have stepped across that line, that indefinable line, beyond which beauty lies. The audience was surprised, startled; this plain-looking girl with the husky voice began to grip it, to gain possession of it. Indeed, her voice had lost its impurity of tone, it had grown warmer and more powerful. When Alfredo appeared, Violetta's cry of joy almost brought forth that storm of applause which goes by the name of *fanatismo*, and beside which all our northern acclamations are as nothing. A moment later, and the audience was plunged in silence again. The duet began, the best thing in the opera: in it the composer has expressed all the regrets of a youth senselessly squandered, the last struggle of hopeless, helpless love. Seized, carried away on a gust of feeling in which all shared, with tears of joy, the artist's joy, and of real suffering in her eyes, she gave herself up to the surge of her emotions; her face was transfigured, and as, confronted by the sudden spectre of approaching death, the words of her impassioned prayer to heaven broke from her: '*Lascia mi vivere . . . morir si giovane*' (Let me live – to die so young) the whole theatre echoed with frantic clapping and rapturous applause.

Elena had turned quite cold. She sought Insarov's hand, held it tight and felt his answering pressure – but neither looked at the other. This time there was a different meaning underlying the caress, a different motive from that which, earlier in the evening, had inspired him to take her hand in the gondola.

They were taken back to the hotel along the Grand Canal. It was a bright mild night. These were the same palaces that glided towards them, but they seemed different now. Those which the moon illuminated shone pale gold, and in that glow the details of the decorations, the outlines of the windows and balconies seemed to disappear; but they stood out more distinctly where the buildings were lightly and evenly overcast with shadow. The gondolas with their small red lamps seemed to move faster and even more noiselessly; with an air of mystery the steel prows glinted, the oars rose and fell over the ripples which were stirred up in the water like so many silver fishes; from all around came the soft, short cries of the gondoliers (nowadays they never sing) and apart from them there was almost no sound at all. The hotel where they were staying was on the Riva degli Schiavoni; but before they reached it they left the gondola and walked several times round the Piazza di San Marco, under the arcades where crowds thronged idly in front of the tiny cafés. There is somehow a peculiar delight in strolling alone with a loved companion in a strange city, among strange people; then everything has charm and significance, and one wishes everyone peace, goodwill and the same happiness that one is enjoying one's self. But Elena was no longer able to give herself up freely to her happiness; her spirit was shaken by all the impressions she had just experienced; while Insarov, as they passed by the Palace of the Doge, silently pointed to the muzzles of the Austrian guns which peered out from beneath the low arches – and pulled his hat over his eyes. Moreover, he was feeling tired; so, with a last look at St Mark's Cathedral, and at its domes, where the moon had set the blue-grey lead aglow with patches of phosphorescent light, they slowly returned home.

Their room looked out on the broad lagoon which stretches from the Riva degli Schiavoni to the Giudecca. Almost opposite their hotel rose the pointed tower of San Giorgio; to the right, high up in the air, shone the golden ball of the Dogana, and the most beautiful of churches, the Redentore of Palladio, stood like a bride adorned; to the left the masts and sail-yards and funnels of ships looked black in the night; a half-spread sail hung like a great wing, with the pennants hardly stirring. Insarov sat down by the window, but Elena did not let him admire the view for long; he had suddenly become feverish, and he was seized with an overpowering feeling of weakness. She put him to bed, and when he was asleep, quietly returned to the window. Oh, how peaceful, how tender the night seemed! The azure air stirred with the softness of a dove; surely all pain, all grief, must needs be silent and sleep beneath the holy, innocent light of that clear sky. 'Oh, God!' thought Elena, 'why must we die, why must we suffer separation and illness and tears? And if we must, then why all this beauty, why this sweet feeling of hope, why this reassuring sense of some lasting refuge, of some safe stronghold, of some immortal guardianship? What then is the meaning of that smiling, beneficent sky, of this earth, so happy and at its ease? Can all this be only what we feel within us – whereas outside, in reality, there is only an eternal icy stillness? Can it be that we are quite alone, alone – while beyond us everywhere there are only fathomless gulfs and chasms in which all is strange to us? Then why this thirst for prayer, why does prayer give us joy? (*"Morir si giovane"* – the words rang in her heart.) May we not entreat for mercy, for help? Oh God, may we not hope for miracles?' She pressed her head to her clenched hands. 'Must it end now?' she whispered, 'must it end already? I have been happy, not for minutes, or hours, or days, but for whole weeks on end. And with what right?' She began to be afraid of her happiness. 'What if we have no right to happiness?' she thought. 'What if happiness has to be paid for? All that was heaven, after all . . . and we are only human beings, poor, sinful human beings . . . *Morir si giovane* . . . Oh, away, dark spectre! It is not only I who needs his life!

'But what if this is a punishment,' she went on. 'What if we are now having to pay in full for our misdeeds? My conscience was quiet, it is quiet, but is that a proof of my innocence? Oh, God, are we such criminals? Do You really mean to punish us because we loved one another – You, who created this night, this sky? If that be so, if he is guilty and I am guilty,' she added with a sudden impulse, 'then, O God, at least grant that he, grant that both of us may die an honourable, glorious death out there on his native fields, and not here, in this lonely room.'

'And your poor, forsaken mother, what of her sorrow?' The question took her aback, and she could not find an answer to it. Elena did not know that every man's happiness is founded on the unhappiness of another, that the comfort and advantage which he enjoys demands, as surely as a statue demands a pedestal, the discomfort and disadvantage of other people.

'Rendich!' muttered Insarov in his sleep.

Elena went up to him on tiptoe, bent over him and wiped the perspiration from his face. He tossed his head on the pillow for a moment, then lay quiet again.

She returned to the window and to her thoughts. She began to persuade herself that there was nothing to fear.

She actually felt ashamed of her own weakness. 'Is there really any danger?' she whispered. 'Isn't he better? After all, if we hadn't gone to the theatre today, all these ideas would never have come into my head.' Just then she saw a white seagull flying high over the water. Probably some fisherman had disturbed it, and now it was swooping noiselessly about, as if looking for some place to settle. 'See if she flies this way,' Elena thought, 'that will be a good sign.' But the gull circled round, folded its wings and sank, with a mournful cry, like a wounded bird behind one of the dark ships. Elena shuddered, then felt ashamed that she had shuddered; without undressing she lay down on the bed beside Insarov, who was breathing heavily and quickly.

XXXIV

INSAROV woke late, with a dull pain in his head and, as he expressed himself, a feeling of 'hideous' weakness all over. However, he got up.

'Hasn't Rendich come?' was his first question.

'Not yet,' Elena replied, and handed him the last issue of the *Osservatore Triestino*, in which there was a great deal of talk about the war, the Slav countries and the Principalities. He had started to read, and she was preparing coffee for him, when there was a knock at the door.

'Rendich,' they both thought: but it was a Russian voice that said: 'May I come in?' They looked at one another wonderingly, but before they had answered, a rather dandified young man, with a small, sharp-featured face and quick eyes, entered the room. He seemed to be radiating self-satisfaction, as though he had just won a lot of money, or heard some excellent news.

Insarov rose in his chair.

'You don't recognize me,' the stranger said, walking up to him jauntily, and bowing amiably to Elena. 'I'm Lupoyarov, you remember we met in Moscow at the E's.'

'Oh, yes, at the E's,' Insarov repeated.

'Of course, of course! Do please introduce me to your wife – madam, I've always had a great respect for Dmitri Vassilyevich, I mean Nikanor Vassilyevich, and I'm very glad to have the honour of meeting you at last. Just think,' he went on, turning to Insarov, 'I only learnt that you were here yesterday. I'm staying in this hotel too. What a place this is, this Venice – poetry, sheer poetry! There's only one awful thing about it, the accursed Austrians wherever you go! – Oh, these Austrians! Incidentally, have you heard that there's been a decisive battle on the Danube – 300 Turkish officers killed? Silistra is taken, and Serbia has declared itself independent. How overjoyed you must be, as a patriot – even I feel my Slav blood tingling! However, I advise you to be careful – I'm sure they've got their eye on you. The spying here is terrible – yesterday some suspicious sort of person came up to me and asked if I was Russian; I said I was a Dane. But really you don't look at all well, my dear Nikanor Vassilyevich. You must look after yourself; madam, you must doctor your husband a little – yesterday I spent running round the churches and palaces – honestly, I was quite beside myself with excitement; you have seen the Palace of the Doge, haven't you? That place is full of treasures! Especially the great gallery, where there's that empty space on the wall for the picture of Marino Falieri, and just the inscription *"Decapitati pro criminibus"*.* I visited the famous prisons too – God! how it made my blood boil! You may remember, I've always been deeply concerned with social questions and up in arms against the aristocracy: well, I'd just like to show the supporters of the aristocracy those prisons. Byron was right when he wrote: "I stood in Venice on the Bridge of Sighs" – of course, he was an aristocrat, too. I've always been for progress, you know; the younger generation is always on the side of progress, isn't it? Well, what do you think of these Anglo–French? We'll just see how much they

* Marino Falieri, a Venetian doge, who was executed in 1355. The space for his portrait, among the portraits of the other doges, was left empty, and provided with the inscription: Here is the space for Falieri, beheaded for his crimes.

manage to achieve, this Boustrapa* and Palmerston; did you know Palmerston has been made Prime Minister? No, whatever you may say, the Russian fist is not to be trifled with. That Boustrapa is a terrible rogue too. Would you like me to let you have a copy of *Les Châtiments* by Victor Hugo? – it's wonderful! *L'avenir le gendarme de Dieu* – how audacious in its brevity, and yet so strong, so strong. Prince Vyazemski has a good thing, too:

> "Europe repeats: Bash-Kadik-Lar:
> But keeps its eyes on Sinope."

Oh, how I love poetry. I've got Proudhon's last book, too – really I've got everything. I don't know how you feel, but I'm glad about this war: however, in case they send for me back to Russia, I'm preparing to leave here for Florence and Rome. France is impossible, so I'm thinking of going to Spain – they say the women are wonderful there, but there's a lot of poverty and vermin. I'd pop over to California, too – nothing's impossible for a Russian – only I promised some editor to make a detailed study of the problem of Mediterranean trade. You may say the subject is dull, a specialist's subject, but that's what we need, we need specialization – we've had enough of philosophizing, now we need something practical, practical . . . But you're looking very unwell, Nikanor Vassilyevich, maybe I'm tiring you; however, I'll just stay a little longer . . .'

For a long time Lupoyarov continued to babble on in this way; and when at last he went away, he promised to call again.

Worn out by this unexpected visitor, Insarov lay down on the sofa.

'There's your younger generation,' he said bitterly,

* Boustrapa, nickname of Napoleon III.

glancing at Elena. 'Some of them may swagger and boast, but at heart they're triflers like this gentleman here.'

Elena did not reply to her husband; at that moment she was far more worried about Insarov's weak condition than about all the younger generation of Russia. She sat down by his side and took up her sewing. He closed his eyes and lay motionless, pale and gaunt. She looked at his haggard profile and his outstretched arms and suddenly fear gripped her heart.

'Dmitri,' she said.

He started.

'What? Has Rendich come?'

'Not yet ... but Dmitri, you're feverish, you're really not at all well, don't you think we should call a doctor?'

'That windbag's scared you. No, it's not necessary. I'll rest a little and it will all pass off. After dinner we'll go out again somewhere.'

Two hours went by; all the while Insarov lay on the sofa, but he was unable to sleep, though he kept his eyes closed. Elena did not leave him; she let her work fall on her lap and sat motionless.

'Why don't you sleep?' she asked, at last.

'Just wait a moment' – he took her hand and laid it under his head. 'There, that's fine. Wake me directly Rendich comes. If he says the boat is ready, we must go immediately. We've all our things to pack.'

'It won't take long to pack,' Elena replied.

'What was that fellow chattering about Serbia and some battle?' he said, after a short pause. 'All invented, I suppose. But we must go, we must go. There's no time to lose – you must be ready.'

He fell asleep; all was quiet in the room. Elena leaned her

head against the back of the arm-chair, and for a long time gazed out of the window. The weather had changed and a wind was blowing. Great white clouds were riding across the sky, the slender masts swayed in the distance, a long pennant bearing a red cross rose and fell, rose and fell unendingly. The old-fashioned clock was ticking away slowly, heavily, with a kind of lugubrious wheeze. Elena closed her eyes; she had slept badly the night before and now she too dozed off.

She had a strange dream. It seemed to her that she was crossing the Tsaritsino lake in a boat with some people she did not know. They were silent and sat quite still; no one was rowing the boat, which moved of its own accord. Elena was not feeling frightened, but she was bored; she wanted to know who these people were and why she was with them. She looked around, and as she did so, the lake grew wider, the banks disappeared; and now it was no longer a lake but a heaving sea, upon whose huge blue, silent waves the boat was rocking with a majestic motion. Some menacing thing seemed to be coming up with a roar from the bottom of the sea; Elena's unknown companions jumped up, shouting and waving their arms ... Elena recognized their faces now; her father was among them. Then a sort of white hurricane burst upon the waters and everything spun round and became confused.

Elena looked about her; it was still white everywhere around, but now it was the whiteness of snow, of endless snow. She was no longer in the boat, but driving in a sledge, just as she had driven away from Moscow, and sitting beside her was a small figure muffled up in an old coat. Elena peered at this new fellow-traveller: it was Katya, the little beggar-girl she had known years ago. Elena began to be afraid: 'Had the child really not died?' she thought.

'Katya, where are we going?'

Katya did not answer, but merely wrapped her coat more closely round her; she was cold . . . Elena was cold also; she looked along the road, and saw in the distance, through the blown snow, the outlines of a city with tall white towers and silver-gleaming cupolas. 'Katya, Katya, is that Moscow? But no,' she thought, 'that's not Moscow, that is the Solovyetsky monastery'; and she knew that in there, in one of its innumerable narrow cells, stuffy and crowded together like the cells of a beehive – in there Dmitri was locked up. 'I must free him.' Suddenly a yawning, grey abyss opened in front of her. The sledge was falling, Katya began to laugh. 'Elena, Elena!' she heard a voice call from the depths.

'Elena!' Now the voice sounded clear and close to her ear. She looked up quickly, turned, and almost fainted at what she saw: Insarov, white as snow, white as the snow of her dream, was half sitting up on the sofa, and looking at her with wide, pale, terrible eyes. His hair was scattered over his brow, his lips parted strangely. Terror, mixed with a sort of yearning tenderness, showed in his suddenly altered features.

'Elena!' he said, 'I am dying.'

With a cry she fell on her knees, and pressed herself to his bosom.

'All is over,' Insarov said, 'I am dying . . . Good-bye, my poor darling! Good-bye my country.'

He fell back on to the sofa.

Elena ran out of the room and called for help; a manservant hurried for a doctor. Elena returned and put her arms around Insarov.

At that moment a man appeared in the doorway. He was broad-shouldered and sunburned, and wore a thick coat and a low-brimmed oilskin hat. He stopped in the doorway, perplexed at what he saw.

'Rendich!' Elena cried. 'You've come! Look, for God's sake look here, he's fainted! What's the matter with him? My God, my God! Yesterday he went out, only a minute ago he was talking to me . . .'

Rendich said nothing, merely standing aside from the doorway: a diminutive person wearing a wig and spectacles promptly slipped past him into the room. It was the doctor, who happened to be living in the same hotel. He went up to Insarov.

'Signora,' he said, after a moment or two, 'the foreign gentleman is dead – *il signore forestiere è morto* – of an aneurism, complicated by disease of the lungs.'

XXXV

THE next day, in that same room, Rendich was standing by the window, while Elena sat before him, wrapped in a shawl. Insarov's body lay in a coffin in the adjoining room. On Elena's face there was a look of lifeless fear; between her eyebrows two deep lines had appeared, which gave a strained expression to her unmoving eyes. On the window-sill lay an opened letter from Anna Vassilyevna. Her mother begged her to come to Moscow, even if only for a month; she complained of her loneliness, she complained of Nikolai Artyomevich; she sent greetings to Insarov, inquired after his health, and begged him to allow his wife to visit her.

Rendich was a Dalmatian, a seaman whom Insarov had got to know during his travels in Bulgaria, and whom he had sought out in Venice. He was a tough, courageous, unpolished fellow, quite devoted to the Slav cause; he despised the Turks and detested the Austrians.

'How long have you to stay in Venice?' Elena asked him in Italian. Her voice was lifeless, like her face.

'A day, so as to load up and not arouse suspicion; then straight back to Zara. This will be bad news for our countrymen. They've been waiting for him a long time; their hopes were set on him.'

'Their hopes were set on him,' Elena repeated mechanically.

'When will you bury him?' he asked.

After a pause she said:

'Tomorrow.'

'Tomorrow? I'll stay. I'd like to throw a handful of earth into his grave. And I must help you too. But it would have been better to bury him in Slav soil.'

Elena glanced at Rendich.

'Captain,' she said, 'take us both with you and land us on the other side of the sea from here. Is it possible?'

Rendich thought for a while.

'It's possible, but it will be hard. There's sure to be difficulties with the accursed officials here . . . But even supposing we managed it, and buried him there, how would I get you back?'

'You won't have to get me back.'

'How do you mean? Where will you stay?'

'I shall find work somewhere; only take us, take us both.'

Rendich scratched the back of his neck.

'As you wish; but it will be very difficult. I'll go and try; you wait for me here in about two hours.'

He went out. Elena crossed into the adjoining room, leaned against the wall, and for a long time stood there as if turned to stone; then she fell on her knees. But Elena was unable to pray; there were no reproaches in her heart; she did not presume to ask God why He had not had mercy or pity on them, why He had not protected them, why He had punished them beyond the measure of their transgression, if indeed it was a transgression. All of us are transgressors, even as we are alive, and there is no thinker so exalted, no human benefactor so great that, by virtue of what he has done for mankind, he may presume that he has the right to live . . . But Elena could not pray; she was turned to stone.

That night a broad-beamed rowing boat left the hotel where the Insarovs had been staying. In it sat Elena and Rendich, and they took with them a long box covered with a black cloth. They were rowed for about an hour, until they reached a small, two-masted vessel which lay at anchor right at the very entrance to the harbour. Elena and Rendich went on board and the sailors carried up the coffin. A storm got up at midnight, but by early morning the ship had already passed the Lido. In the course of the day the storm began to rage with frightful ferocity, and experienced seamen in Lloyd's office shook their heads and expected to hear bad news: between Venice, Trieste and the Dalmatian coast the Adriatic is extraordinarily dangerous.

Three weeks after Elena had left Venice, Anna Vassilyevna received the following letter in Moscow:

My dearest parents,

I am writing to say good-bye to you for ever; you will not see me again. Yesterday Dmitri died and everything is finished for me. Today I am taking his body to Zara. I shall bury him and then I do not know what will become of me. But I no longer have any other country than Dmitri's own, and there they are getting ready for rebellion and war; I shall join the Sisters of Mercy and look after the sick and wounded. I do not know what will become of me, but now that Dmitri is dead I shall remain true to his memory, and to the cause which he followed all his life. I have learnt Bulgarian and Serbian. Probably I shall not survive all this – so much the better. I have been brought to the edge of an abyss and I must go down into it. Fate did not unite us for nothing; who knows, perhaps I killed him; now it is his turn to call me after him. I sought happiness, perhaps I shall find death. Maybe that is as it should be, it may be that I have done wrong. But isn't it true that death heals everything and brings reconciliation to all? Forgive me the grief I have caused you; it was not of my willing. But as for returning to Russia – why? What is there to do in Russia?

Take my last kiss and blessing and do not condemn me.

E.

* * *

Since then nearly five years have passed, and there has been no more news of Elena. All letters and inquiries have been fruitless; and Nikolai Artyomevich, after the conclusion of the peace, travelled to Venice and Zara in vain. In Venice he learnt only what the reader already knows, and in Zara no one could give him any definite information about Rendich or about the ship which he had hired. There were vague rumours that some years back, after a severe storm, the sea had cast up on to the shore a coffin, in which had been found the remains of a man. According to other, more reliable reports, the coffin was not thrown up by the sea at all, but had been brought there by a foreign lady from Venice, and buried by the shore; some said that this lady had been seen afterwards in Herzogovina with the army which was being raised there at the time; they even described her dress, which they said was black from head to foot. However that may be, all trace of Elena has vanished for ever and beyond recall, and no one knows whether she still lives in hiding somewhere, or whether she has already played out her small part in life – whether that ferment of the spirit is at rest at last, and the turn of death has come.

Sometimes a man will wake up with an involuntary shudder and ask himself: 'Can I indeed be thirty . . . or forty . . . or fifty years old? How is it possible that life has passed so quickly? How is it possible that death has come so near?' But death is like a fisherman who, having caught a fish in his net, leaves it in the water for a time; the fish continues to swim about, but all the while the net is round it, and the fisherman will snatch it out in his own good time.

* * *

What became of the other characters in our story? Anna Vassilyevna is still alive; she has seemed much older since the blow struck her, she complains less, but she grieves far more. Nikolai Artyomevich also seems much older, and his hair has turned grey. He has parted with Avgustina Christianovna; now he abuses everything foreign. His housekeeper, a good-looking Russian woman of about thirty, dresses in silk and wears gold rings on her fingers and gold ear-rings. Kurnatovski, as a man not without human passions, and also as an admirer of pretty blondes (being one of the dark, energetic sort himself) has married Zoya; she is very obedient to him, and has even given up thinking in German. Bersyenev is in Heidelberg; he went abroad on a state grant and visited Berlin and Paris. He is not wasting his time and will make a sound professor; the learned public has already noticed two articles he has published: *On certain peculiarities of ancient German law in regard to judicial punishment*, and *On the significance of the urban principle in the problem of civilization*. It is only regrettable that both articles are written in a rather heavy style and over-weighted with foreign words.

Shubin is in Rome. He has given himself up wholly to his art and is reckoned one of the most notable and promising of the younger sculptors. Critical visitors take the view that he has not sufficiently studied the classics, that he lacks 'style'; they regard him as belonging to the French School. He has a great many commissions on hand from English and American patrons. Recently a *Bacchante* of his caused a great stir, and the well-known Russian Count Boboshkin, a man of great wealth, was on the point of paying 1,000 scudi for it; but he ultimately preferred to pay 3,000 to another sculptor, a pure-blooded Frenchman, for a group representing 'A peasant girl dying of love on the bosom of the Spirit of Spring'. Shubin occasionally corresponds with Uvar Ivanovich, who alone has not changed in any way. 'Do you remember,' he wrote not long ago, 'what you said to me the night we heard of poor Elena's marriage, and I was sitting on your bed talking to you? You remember I asked you when we should have some real people among us, and you replied "They'll come." Oh, spirit of the black earth! Today, from my pleasant remoteness, I am writing to ask you once again: "How about it, Uvar Ivanovich, are they coming?"'

Uvar Ivanovich, reading that letter, waggled his fingers and gazed cryptically into the distance.

APPENDIX

THE ORIGIN OF 'ON THE EVE'

As has been mentioned in the introduction to this volume, the plan of *On the Eve* was formed in Turgenev's mind long before he began to write the story. His original conception was the character of Elena. 'The figure of the principal heroine, then still a new type, was fairly clearly outlined in my imagination,' he recalled afterwards; 'but a hero was lacking, a person of such a character that Elena, with her powerful though still vague yearning for freedom, could abandon herself to him.' Postponed for a time, the fulfilment of the plan was ultimately brought about in rather curious circumstances.

During Turgenev's 'exile' in Spasskoye, a frequent visitor at his house was the twenty-five-year-old Vassili Karatyeev, a neighbouring landowner, and a former student of Moscow University. Karatyeev was unpopular with the gentry on account of 'his free-thinking and his mocking tongue', and also his reputation as a dangerous ladies' man; Turgenev, however, described him as a romantic enthusiast, with a great love of literature and music, and an original sense of humour. Later, at the time of the Crimean War, the local landowners elected Karatyeev for military service, having agreed among themselves to get rid of him; but before he went away to the war he handed Turgenev a small note-book containing some fifteen pages of manuscript, with the request that the novelist should read it and make something of it, so that 'if he were lost, it would not be without trace'.

Telling the story of this episode, Turgenev said that he was going to refuse, but seeing that a refusal would distress his friend, promised to carry out his wish. 'That evening, after Karatyeev's departure, I read through the note-book,' Turgenev goes on; 'in it I found roughly sketched out what afterwards formed the subject of *On the Eve*, though the story was not completed and broke off abruptly. Karatyeev while in Moscow had become enamoured of a young woman who at first returned his love; later, however, she got to know a Bulgarian named Katranov . . . fell in love with him and went away with him to Bulgaria, where he soon died. The story of this love was sincerely but clumsily recorded in the note-book; Karatyeev, indeed, was not born a writer. Only one scene, namely the journey to Tsaritsino, was depicted fairly vividly and I retained its main features. . . . Reading through Karatyeev's note-book I cried involuntarily: "that's the hero I've been looking for!"'

Not much is known of this Bulgarian, the real-life prototype of Turgenev's Insarov. As a youth he was a student of Moscow University where much was hoped of him by the local Bulgarian colony; later he developed tuberculosis, went to Vienna for treatment, and died in Venice while still young. In sharp contrast to the hero of the novel, who was without artistic sensibility, Katranov was a poet, and had had both original work and translations published.

It is said that Karatyeev, the author of the manuscript, was the original of another character in the novel, that of Shubin. In this connection, however, it is worth recalling that Turgenev strongly repudiated the view, held by many of his contemporaries, that he merely 'copied' his characters from his real-life acquaintances. He believed that the task of the writer was not to present portraits of his friends, but to create artistic types.

MORE ABOUT PENGUINS
AND PELICANS

For further information about books available from Penguins please write to Dept EP, Penguin Books Ltd, Harmondsworth, Middlesex UB7 0DA.

In the U.S.A.: For a complete list of books available from Penguins in the United States write to Dept CS, Penguin Books, 625 Madison Avenue, New York, New York 10022.

In Canada: For a complete list of books available from Penguins in Canada write to Penguin Books Canada Ltd, 2801 John Street, Markham, Ontario L3R 1B4.

In Australia: For a complete list of books available from Penguins in Australia write to the Marketing Department, Penguin Books Australia Ltd, P.O. Box 257, Ringwood, Victoria 3134.

In New Zealand: For a complete list of books available from Penguins in New Zealand write to the Marketing Department, Penguin Books (N.Z.) Ltd, P.O. Box 4019, Auckland 10.

DOSTOYEVSKY

Crime and Punishment

When Dostoyevsky began, in 1865, to write the novel that was to bring him international recognition he was as embarrassed with debts as the hero he created. Raskolnikov, an impoverished student, decides to murder a stupid and grasping old woman for gain. After the murder he is unable to tolerate his growing sense of guilt. This universal theme is one which had preoccupied the author during his own imprisonment in Siberia.

The Idiot

Perhaps the most appealing of all Dostoyevsky's heroes, Prince Myshkin, the Idiot, is in one view the pure idealized Christian and in another the catalyst of a bitter criticism of the Russian ruling class. This dual vision marks out for the modern reader *The Idiot* as one of Dostoyevsky's major novels.

The Brothers Karamazov

Dostoyevsky completed *The Brothers Karamazov*, the culmination of his work, in 1880 shortly before his death. This profound story of parricide and fraternal jealousy involves the questions of anarchism, atheism and the existence of God.

The Devils

This political drama, the most controversial of his masterpieces, has been both hailed as a grim prophecy of the Russian Revolution and denounced as the work of a reactionary. It is a penetrating commentary on men and affairs as well as a work of tragic intensity in which the recesses of the mind and the dark passions of men are probed.

All volumes translated by David Magarshack

Also published in translations by Jessie Coulson:

THE GAMBLER/BOBOK/A NASTY STORY
NOTES FROM UNDERGROUND *and* THE DOUBLE

TOLSTOY

War and Peace (Two volumes)

Few would dispute the claim of *War and Peace* to be regarded as the greatest novel in any language. This massive chronicle, to which Tolstoy devoted five whole years shortly after his marriage, portrays Russian family life during and after the Napoleonic war.

Anna Karenin

In this masterpiece of humanity Tolstoy depicts the tragedy of a fashionable woman who abandons husband, son and social position for a passionate liaison which finally drives her to suicide. We are also given a true reflection of Tolstoy himself in the character of Levin and his search for the meaning of life.

Childhood, Boyhood, Youth

These semi-autobiographical sketches, published in Tolstoy's early twenties, provide an expressive self-portrait in which one may discern the man and the writer he was to become.

The Cossacks/Ivan Ilyich/Happy Ever After

The three stories in this volume illustrate different aspects of Tolstoy's knowledge of human nature.

Resurrection

Tolstoy's last novel reveals the teeming underworld of Russian society; the rotten heart of his country.

All volumes translated by Rosemary Edmonds

HENRY TROYAT
Tolstoy

'Nothing less than this magnificent, massive, 700-page biography could even begin to do justice to one of the most complex, baffling and grand men that ever lived . . . a masterly book. M. Troyat would have to be invented if he did not exist as the ideal biographer' – *Sunday Telegraph*

TURGENEV

SKETCHES FROM A HUNTER'S ALBUM

TRANSLATED BY RICHARD FREEBORN

For most of its present-day readers Turgenev's early masterpiece is quite simply one of the most beautiful books in any language: a lyrical, almost magical account of wanderings in the Russian countryside, to read which is an unforgettable experience. Yet when it was published in 1852 it was regarded by Tsarist officialdom as a subversive work which appeared to denounce the whole Russian social system. Perhaps the secret behind this apparent contradiction lies in that combination of urbanity, compassion, and intellect which is Turgenev's special genius. Condemning nothing, he reveals the peasants of his beloved country as individual human beings, suffering and oppressed in what might have been a paradise.

Also published:

FATHERS AND SONS
Translated by Rosemary Edmonds

HOME OF THE GENTRY
Translated by Richard Freeborn

RUDIN
Translated by Richard Freeborn

FIRST LOVE
Translated by Isaiah Berlin
and introduced by V. S. Pritchett

THE PENGUIN CLASSICS

A selection

Cicero
MURDER TRIALS *Michael Grant*

DEMOSTHENES AND AESCHINES *A. N. W. Saunders*

Stendhal
LOVE *Gilbert and Suzanne Sale*

Alarcón
THE THREE-CORNERED HAT *M. Alpert*

Maupassant
BEL-AMI *Douglas Parmée*

Corneille
THE CID/CINNA/THE THEATRICAL ILLUSION
J. Cairncross

BIRDS THROUGH A CEILING OF ALABASTER: THREE ABBASID
POETS *G. B. H. Wightman and A. Y. al-Udhari*

Livy
ROME AND THE MEDITERRANEAN *Henry Bettenson and
A. H. MacDonald*

LIVES OF THE LATER CAESARS *Anthony Birley*

Flaubert
BOUVARD AND PECUCHET *A. K. Krailsheimer*